SUMMER of ANTOINETTE

SUMMER of ANTOINETTE

a novel by
Pete Trudgeon

Dot Screen Studios

Detroit

The characters and events in this book are fictional. Any similarity to persons living or dead is purely coincidental and not intended by the author.

© 2013 by Pete Trudgeon. All rights reserved.

Published by Dot Screen Studios.

Book design and illustrations by Mike Ortiz.

For Nastia, sneak thief of my imagination

Foreword

I'd abandoned guilt. My parents, father Ronald, mother Margret while alive were not religious. Yet, on the right breast of the grey blazers that my younger sister and I wore during our 12 years of formal education bore the insignia of Our Lady of the Blessed Virgin. I suppose sending us to a private institution, staffed by priests and nuns, practiced in a faith no one in my family held, was an attempt to bestow in us a sense of structured morality. Like most good intentions it was doomed to fail. Spending so much time in such a fetishistic environment allowed time for many a seed to be planted.

Over the years I'd been forced to listen to the long held complaints of former students from identical schools. Their laments are always identical whining of rigid structure, the occasional corporal punishment (wooden paddles on the backside) and lack of individuality. I, on the other hand, enjoyed my environment and have fond memories. I even volunteered my services as altar boy for the once a week, Wednesday morning mass. I liked the way the priest's orations echoed off the church's stone walls, the sound of the organ and the glow of lit candles. I felt a participant in an ancient and somewhat mysterious rite. Above me the large crucifix with the figure of Jesus attached by nails, sad eyes staring backward, and in front of me were row after row of my female classmates; dozens of pairs of knees rosy from kneeling. The way their moist tongues pushed out to receive the paper thin wafer, meant to represent the flesh of their lord and savior.

Still, there was nothing in my upbringing that would lead me to believe I'd one day hold the thoughts towards, or commit the acts I'd perpetrate with Antoinette Mouse. Antoinette Mouse: young in body, ancient in soul. She who purified me through corruption. I've come to an understanding regarding this mysterious thing we call desire, unpredictable in its arrival, triggered by a photograph, a scent, or a gesture such as a young girl lifting her hair so that she may rub the back of her neck. In other words, a thousand such things. It leads one on a journey, often lonely, where you know neither the length of the road nor what is behind the bend until its been turned. You are hungry, but not fed, you thirst, but are not quenched.

My history with females had two commonalities. Most accused me of keeping secrets, and fate always conspired to, at one point, rob me of their company. First was Michele Alberts who bestowed upon me my first kiss. It happened on a cold February afternoon during kindergarten recess. She was followed by Lisa Wheeler, my babysitter and first love. She will be discussed in detail later.

As the years passed, they came in this order: Barbara Looker, elementary school temptress and completely unobtainable. Joyce Laurent who lost her virginity to me at age 16 in her parent's basement. There are more, their faces and bodies are faded images floating in my memory, only their names are clear: Jennifer, Ami, Maureen, Regina, a few others. But with the exception of my dear Lisa, none stir any gentle nostalgia or harsh regret, and with the arrival of Antoinette they'd finally be transformed into the hollow couplings they'd always been.

Part One
MAY

Chapter One

I'd recently returned to America to bury my family, mother, father, and little sister Alison. I'd been living in Italy when I received the news of their deaths. A plane crash, they'd been on their way to visit me.

To my late parent's relief I'd finally secured employment after a long period of idleness. It'd come to me purely by chance while attending a dinner party. There I met Passolini Salo, a film director who'd gained notoriety for specializing in the horror genre. He was a large man, but carried himself with such ease and swiftness in his movements that one never thought of him as fat or slovenly. His tight salt and pepper curls were swept back and his eyes were always hidden behind amber lenses. To this day, I'm ignorant of their true color.

His English proved better than my Italian and our initial conversation was flavored by alcohol and scented by his large Cuban cigar. Passolini's films were structured around a half dozen gruesome set pieces. I'd let an idea fall, a variation on the 'Black Dahlia' murder, which appealed to his taste for the macabre.

I'd begun writing as a hobby since childhood, graduated as an English major, but after I'd taken it up professionally, I'd found it difficult to completely devote myself seriously. As a result, my income had been sporadic at best. I was either flush or dead broke.

When I did work I wrote for various music publications, mostly I covered up-and-coming American rock bands as they toured overseas. My articles were sanitized records of backstage debauchery. I grew to intensely dislike musicians and became bored with their world. After abandoning my career as a journalist, I gathered what savings I'd managed to accrue and spent the past 18 months traveling through Europe.

I'd bought a secondhand camera and had begun to dabble in photography. I'd been told by a few people that I had a good eye.

Passolini had been so taken by my scenario he asked me to read the script he was about to shoot and offer any suggestions I had on how it could be improved. I accepted his offer and found much wanting. This resulted in my being hired as a rewrite man. After that film's completion Passolini offered to keep me on, he was already preparing his next project. But the sudden death of my family made remaining in Europe impossible. America was calling. I had obligations. We'd finally come to an agreement that once my affairs were in order I'd begin work on the new script. We'd communicate by phone until he arrived in the States.

Chapter Two

The return home turned out to be less stressful than I'd originally anticipated. There were meetings with my parent's attorney where condolences and cups of coffee were offered before I lent my signature to the numerous documents that required it. Then there was the funeral, all three were buried at the Olive Cemetery, in family plots that had been bought a decade previous. The weather during the ceremony was, as my mother would have noted, pleasant, sunny and cloudless. It was attended by what few relatives I had, and family friends. Some I recognized, most I didn't. If anyone was angered by my status as sole heir they didn't voice it. All of their faces have since vanished from my memory along with their kind words and wreathes of flowers. The only thing that lingered was the sickeningly sweet smell of those bouquets. Once my loved ones were put to rest I immediately set about getting reacquainted with my childhood home.

My father made his money from inheritance and his work as a corporate lawyer. He'd purchased the property when the area was still mostly wilderness and scattered farms. He worked in the city and had long made up his mind not to live there, even though this decision came with a daily commute of over an hour both ways. This was before they expanded the freeway system. This also meant the school we attended, the aforementioned Blessed Virgin, was nearly forty miles from our front door. There we walked the halls and inhabited classrooms with the children of families who lived within walking distance of Lake St. Clair. Old money, Alison and I were considered 'country' and treated as such. Nothing stated openly, there were other ways to show condemnation. Those children would've never considered traveling to us, and we were similarly disinterested. We were without peers in our immediate surroundings as well. As a result, Alison and I had only each other for companionship.

By the time we'd reached our early teens civilization had already encroached, but our home remained surrounded by a natural barrier of trees so it retained a quality of still being somewhat isolated. Unseen from the road with only a modest brick transom at the foot of the driveway and a mailbox with our address stenciled on its side as clues to its existence. The house was set back behind a front yard that was kept in year-long shade. Our mother sometimes complained of what she considered the gloominess of this front exterior, but our father would never entertain the notion of taking down a single tree. As a compromise he made the backyard open and the sun was indulged. Alison and I were quite happy, especially with the lot to the left of the house. Despite numerous and generous offers from developers my father refused to sell it and so it remained untouched. It was in these woods we spent many days of our childhood within the trees and in our wandering imaginations.

Although we were not twins, Alison was two years younger than I we were often mistaken as such. Both of us had the same straw blonde hair, pale blue eyes and fair skin. Adults often complimented us on our reserved manner, our disinterest in their patter was taken as good manners on our part. Unknown to even our parents, Alison and I had managed to develop our own form of silent communication. We seemed to be of one mind instead of two, this extended to the physical.

It first happened when I was 15 Alison had newly reached her thirteenth year. Our parents had made arrangements to visit out of state friends for the weekend and had pronounced us old enough to be responsible for our own well-being. Naturally, we were thrilled with our upcoming independence, though, outwardly we behaved nonchalant.

Friday morning arrived and we bid our parents goodbye and wished them a safe journey. The rest of the day passed uneventfully. Our only indulgence was staying up past midnight and watching "Beyond the Door" on television. But by the following afternoon the weather had begun to sour, and by nightfall the wind had kicked up with such force that it bent the trees sideways. It was followed by a fierce thunder storm. Our house was continuously hit by waves of thick pellets of rain, the sound reminded me of a machine gun being fired.

Unlike me, Alison had always harbored a deep fear of these storms and couldn't stand to be by herself when one was raging. As a small child she'd seek comfort by crawling into bed with my parents, but the practice had been discouraged as she'd gotten older. That night she sought solace by quietly entering my room and sliding beside me. It hadn't been the first occasion and normally my presence was enough for her to fall quickly asleep. But this evening Alison seemed even more agitated than usual. She wrapped her arms around me and I felt her shivering as she hugged her body closer to mine. I stroked her hair while whispering assurances in her ear, this seemed to calm her, but as our bodies remained pressed together I began to feel a strange warmth emerge from inside me and I began to entertain unnatural ideas. There had been times when we were alone together, our knees accidentally touching, our eyes lingering. Alison sometimes would leave her bedroom door open, wide enough for me to catch a revealing glimpse and there were occasions I felt she was provoking my gaze.

When I lifted her chin and put my lips on hers she didn't resist me, instead she encouraged me to proceed further. We took things to their conclusion. I remember waking up the next morning, naked in each other's arms, shafts of dusty sunlight came through the windows.

That would not be the last time we'd share such intimacy. It would always occur spontaneously and was never discussed afterwards. I'd always wondered, but never sought out an answer to a pair of questions. Did our parents have knowledge of that night's storm, and did they consciously keep it from us?

Chapter Three

Aside from my assignment for Passolini my life was rather idle. Being the sole heir I was in no need of earning a living. In a matter of weeks I'd transformed into somewhat of a hermit, neither speaking, nor seeing anyone except for Passolini and the man I'd hired to mow the lawn every other week. I'd venture out to buy groceries and once went to a movie, but my obligations and desires remained modest.

At some point I'd began a ritual of taking extended walks around the property. I'd start our just before dusk and brought along a flashlight to help guide me after dark. These strolls served a dual purpose of either working out a script problem or simply clearing my head. On several occasions I became overcome with the feeling I was being watched. I'd always attributed it to an animal, perhaps a stray cat or a raccoon, even deer were not an uncommon sight. It was only much later, upon reflection that I considered that this voyeur was human.

Chapter Four

Thursday, May 25, that was the day I first met Antoinette Mouse. I'd taken to writing outdoors on the backyard patio. The weather had been warm, but not oppressively so, there'd even been gentle breezes that kiss the back of my neck. After a few hours I'd decided to take a break and had stopped inside to take a bottle of beer from the refrigerator. I'd returned to my seat and was nursing the drink when out of the corner of my eye I spotted Antoinette.

She was standing behind a tree. How long she'd been there silently observing me I'd never know, but when our eyes met she smiled and stepped out from behind the cover. As she silently approached me, I took the opportunity to contemplate her. Her hair was a sun-bleached mop whose ends curled around her face, her lower lip had a pout that hinted mischief. She wore a light brown halter top and cut-off jeans, clothing that did little to conceal that Antoinette's body had bloomed early and her flawless skin had already begun turning a caramel color. She was barefoot, a pair of brown leather sandals dangled from the fingers of her left hand. But her most profound feature were her eyes: blue like a tropic sky. Striking, even at a distance, so ungodly beautiful they shouldn't have existed. Yet they did. They looked at me, held me.

'Hello, my name is Antoinette Mouse.' She said it without a trace of embarrassment of being discovered, uninvited on a stranger's property. On the contrary she behaved quite at home. Antoinette held out her hand, I took it without question and felt heat radiating from her palm. Once I let go she sat down in the chair across from me and tossed her sandals on the ground. Within seconds of that first encounter I'd already felt the rush of blood below my waist. As Antoinette stretched out her legs she resumed speaking. 'I'm spending the summer with my aunt. Perhaps you know her, Miss Christine Fairfield, she lives five houses down, she said, pointing to the left with her thumb.

Although the name was vaguely familiar I couldn't conjure a mental picture of the woman.

'We may have met, but it was probably years ago. I've just recently returned after living abroad for several years.'

Antoinette's eyebrows went up slowly, 'Where exactly?'

'London briefly, but the weather was dreary so I went and stayed in Paris for a month. But most of my time was spent in Italy.'

She lifted her right leg and began to scratch her knee, 'I've visited some foreign countries with my parents. Nowhere glamorous like you, though, mostly places where they haven't yet discovered indoor plumbing. What are you writing?'

I'd forgotten the pile of papers in front of me. 'A film script.'

Antoinette leaned forward, enough for me to catch a glimpse of her cleavage. 'What's it about?'

'A homicidal maniac who kills college co-eds with a chainsaw, not exactly the thing that'll lead to an Oscar nomination,' I said, suddenly feeling embarrassed.

'I quite like horror movies, especially British ones from the fifties and sixties. I think Christopher Lee is even a better Dracula than Bela Lugosi.'

'I agree. It's too bad they don't make films like that anymore.' I couldn't help but wonder, who was this Antoinette Mouse, this tanned sprite who showed up in my backyard and spoke to me with the casualness of an old friend? I'd began having a series of lurid thoughts and was grateful for the table that concealed my lower body. Antoinette had repositioned herself so that her legs were draped over the arm of the chair when something grabbed her attention and made her scowl.

'Would you just look at the state of my feet,' she said as she grabbed her right foot and pulled it up toward her face. I noticed they were both grey with dirt, but I found this adorable instead of repulsive.

She released her foot and grinned slightly, 'Aunt Christine doesn't like me going barefoot, says it's something only tomboys do. She can be so funny sometimes. Still, I suppose I should wash up. Mind if I use that hose over there?' She pointed at the hose coiled like a green serpent at the side of the house.

'Go right ahead.'

Antoinette rose from the chair, she picked up her sandles and walked to the spicket. Seconds later water was pouring from the hoses mouth. She tested it on her fingers.

'Cold,' she stated before she proceeded to thoroughly wash both feet. When she'd finished she shut the hose off and slipped on her sandles. It was then I noticed the remains of red polish on her toenails. For some reason it caused a fresh wave of excitement within me.

Antoinette returned to her seat, suddenly she appeared chagrined. 'How terribly rude of me, I haven't even asked you your name.'

I hadn't noticed myself until then. 'Matthew. Matthew Dante.'

Again, she leaned forward, her elbow rested on her leg, her chin resting in the palm of her hand. 'Well, Matthew Dante, I hope you can forgive my boorish behavior, it seems I still have a way to go on the road to maturity.'

'Consider it granted.'

Newly forgiven, her curiosity returned. 'So what do you do when not writing movies?'

'I spend a great deal of time being lazy.'

Antoinette brushed some hair from her cheek, 'Nothing wrong with being lazy. I'm quite good at it myself.' She flashed me another smile and then stood up. 'I've had a very nice time visiting with you, Matthew, hope you don't mind if I stop by again.'

'Not at all.' I hadn't said something with such honesty in months.

Antoinette gave me one more little smile before she turned to walk away.

'Antoinette,' I half shouted. She stopped and looked over her shoulder.

'How old are you? My question inspired another grin, not so innocent.

'Fifteen.' It sounded like a dare.

For the remainder of the day I replayed my first encounter with Antoinette, examined certain moments, her gestures and changes in facial expression. I dwelled over her golden brown skin, what it would be like to run my hand across one of her legs, starting at the inner thigh, my palm running down the entire length to her ankle. Would it feel warm, like her hand when it had briefly clasped mine? Then there were those eyes that had penetrated me. What had she seen while she'd clandestinely observed me?

She had behaved with such ease, there hadn't been the usual apprehension I'd noticed in girls her age alone in the presence of an adult male. I'd noticed this same relaxed manner in some of the European girls I'd encountered, particularly the French, who thought nothing of walking the beaches in the skimpiest of swim suits, apparently ignorant of their effect on the leering teenage boys. Of course, I'd known it was a pose, the majority of them were completely aware of the maddening intoxication they left in their wake.

Strangely, in my entire time abroad I'd remained almost completely chaste. There'd been a lone exception, a twenty-year-old who'd been backpacking her way across Europe. It'd been a one-night stand induced by a couple bottles of wine. I found myself unable to recall in any great detail either the encounter or the girl.

After hours of this frustration I gave in to my baser instincts and went to my bedroom to seek some release. It took but minutes and did nothing to quell the fire that had been lit.

Chapter Five

Antoinette did return, five days later. I'd already developed a callous on my right hand. She had an uncanny gift for stealth. Her arrivals came silently. I wouldn't become aware of her presence until after my pen was set down. There she would be, mere feet away, sitting in the same chair silently observing. She wore tee shirts of pink, yellow, blue, thin white blouses with short sleeves and two top buttons undone. And always those cut-offs, faded, worn fringed edges, one more washing and they'd disintegrate. Tawny skin wrapped in a form that curved in all the right places. I'd taken to keeping a mental record of her skin tone, how much it darkens with each visit. In comparison was her hair, gold and silken.

Our conversations were pleasant exchanges of trivial occurrences, such as the new bathing suit bought for her by her aunt.

'My first two-piece, which my mother would never approve of. It's funny, considering I've overheard her brag to her friends about how she'd danced topless in Golden Gate Park. Of course, that was long before I was born.'

In other instances she'd report on her latest discoveries concerning her new environment, the neighbors, their habits, and minor scandals. I was informed of her aunt's pronounced drinking habit, and of the man she was seeing.

'His name's Charlie, and he's a complete dunce.'

She'd inquire on how my script was progressing. I'd sometimes ask her to read some pages then ask her opinion about a plot point or line of dialogue. Antoinette would pause before answering, carefully considering her words. Her responses often surprised me with their insightfulness, and I found myself using her suggestions.

More than once she steered our conversation towards the state of my love life, always acting as if it was the first time the topic had been raised. After her departure I'd be struck with how much personal information she'd extracted. Meanwhile, Antoinette, herself, remained somewhat a mystery.

Often, I found my mind drifting and images would be conjured. Antoinette in her bikini, lying on a towel, her skin slick with suntan oil. I'd recall a previous visit, her sitting at the edge of the unused fish pond, eating blueberries and showing me her stained fingers. Drops of condensation on a glass of lemonade falling and splashing against her bare thigh. Or those rare forays out, I'd see her about the neighborhood, on the front lawn of her aunt's home, on a street corner as she waited for the light to change, she'd see me, then smile and wave. It was always as if she'd been expecting me.

I'd come to a realization, of having stumbled into a territory I found both wonderful and terrifying. My previous experiences with females had been, with the exception of Alison, rather ordinary, and always within my age group. I'd been in the presence of adolescent girls, with their thin, flat forms, their faces that went instantly from giggles to frown. Never had I ever felt even the merest tinge of wanting towards one of those immature creatures.

Antoinette was a completely different incarnation. Yes, her darling face was the very portrait of girlish innocence, but below the neck she was fully matured. She was a living paradox, a taboo made flesh. That she was forbidden only increased my dreadful desire for her. I felt the beast stir, weakly did I battle it.

Every man is exposed to at least one tender trap in the course of their years. While they may give in to a fleeting fancy of the mind, they just as quickly return to their senses feeling both fortunate and cheated. Antoinette inspired obscenity, the lecher inside me. She was such pretty poison.

Chapter Six

Passolini had phoned me with the news he'd arrived in America and informed me that I could continue work on the script without haste, he was still haggling over the budget with his producers. Towards the end of our conversation he'd remarked that I sounded preoccupied. Indeed I had been, Antoinette was dancing in my head.

This next statement took me by surprise, 'Matthew, you sound as if you're in love.'

'I am, dangerously so.'

Chapter Seven

I'd set my pen down and had proceeded to doze off. When I awoke I'd found Antoinette sitting in her usual spot. She'd been watching me sleep.

'Hello sleepyhead.'

She wore a pale green cotton top, the front of which was held closed by cross-hatched drawstrings. It plunged into a deep V down to her naval. It seemed positively criminal. I could tell by the expression that came across her face that something was bothering her.

'Is something the matter?' I asked

'David Hersh,' she responded as she kicked off her sandles.

'Who's David Hersh?'

She frowned. 'A boy who just told me he likes me.'

That wasn't a surprise, I'd expected the neighborhood boys to foster crushes towards her.

'Do you like him?'

Her expression went from soured to shocked.

'No, he picks his nose and smells odd. Why would such a disgusting person be attracted to me?'

I really didn't believe she didn't know the answer already. Still, I offered, 'The same reason a fly is drawn to honey, because it's sweet.'

Antoinette smiled and looked down at her feet. Had that been a blush I saw redden her face, was she actually capable of shy moments? She raised her head, rubbed her cheek against her shoulder. 'So, you think I'm sweet, do you think I'm pretty?' She asked oh so coyly under her breath.

'I think you're quite beautiful.' It left my mouth too quickly and I'd begun to feel uneasy.

'So, you like me,' came out a statement instead of a question.

I didn't get a chance to respond, Antoinette got up and slid into my lap. The beast was wide awake. She wrapped her arms around my neck, her twin sapphires fixed. Then, after she nipped her lower lip, she leaned in and whispered into my ear, 'Matthew, I've seen the way you look at me.' Key inserted into lock.

My hands were still firmly on the chair.

'I liked it.'

The key turned.

That first kiss, wet, tasted like bubble gum. When my hands came up to embrace her I realized her shirt had no back, my fingers felt bare spine, then shoulders, and I pressed her closer.

The door opened.

I felt my pulse quicken as her tongue darted into my mouth, each kiss lingered a moment longer and our breathing became fervid. When I felt Antoinette's hand reach down and touch the wakened beast I heard myself inhale sharply. That delicate hand within reach of my appalling instrument.

'Don't worry, I'm not a virgin.'

Antoinette rose up she took me by the hand and led me inside, as if she knew her destination by instinct. I knew what was about to happen. It could be argued I was fully capable of preventing it. I didn't put up even the weakest of resistance. I didn't want to. What man puts a stop to what he's been dreaming of, even if that dream is despicable?

That was the day I became a deviant.

I wanted Antoinette, a little girl. The child turned out to have an appetite. I'd been with females nearly twice her age who weren't nearly so aware of themselves or their bodies' cravings. Antoinette was happy to give pleasure, happier when taking it. Antoinette above me, biting her pout, emitting tiny gasps, smiling at my body's final convulsions.

'Don't worry, I'm not a virgin.'

Indeed. I may as well have been. Afterward, her head resting on my chest, me covered in girl scent. I hear her voice, 'Now, we're each other's secret.'

It was the sound of triumph.

Later, when we stood under the shower the sight of soapy water running down the small of Antoinette's back reawakened the beast. She indulged it. After Antoinette departed, she had to be home for dinner, and with the memory of her body stretched across my mattress I finally permitted myself the time to consider what had happened.

How long had she been planning my seduction, and how had she been so certain it would be successful? It's always after consummation that questions come. I felt exhaustion creep over me and allowed myself to lose another battle. I believe that, just before I lost consciousness, in some dark corner of my mind that there would be consequences. Their origin proved to be from a then unknown source.

Chapter Eight

Later that week while attending to some business in town I ran into Mitchell Ortiz, a friend from my university days. It'd been years since we'd seen each other. Aside from a slight weight gain he seemed the same as remembered, vague as that memory was.

We ended up at an outdoor café, over drinks Mitchell brought me up to date on the comings and goings of mutual friends. As he spoke I found myself not entirely engaged. During my entire time abroad I hadn't bothered to keep in contact with anyone, nor had I missed their companionship. I'd recently come to the conclusion that when one is young and finding their way they need friends. But at my then age of 26 these relationships had become just another bothersome hobby.

I'd also come to realize, with increasing frequency, that I had been having difficulty remembering names and faces. It seemed that every other name Mitchell dropped drew a blank. After I'd returned stateside I'd come across a box of photographs, although I appeared in a majority of them I couldn't recall the occasion or the reason it had been deemed worthy of documenting. Before we parted Mitchell mentioned an upcoming engagement party, the couple's names were Catherine Lime and Anthony Marshall. When he asked if I'd planned to attend I lied and said yes. My memory had once again failed me. Of course, I wouldn't have gone anyway, I'd always disliked anything connected with weddings. As I watched Mitchell disappear into the distance I knew even then that would be the last time I'd ever see him. It didn't bother me in the least

After I'd returned home I received a phone call from Passolini. He'd finally settled his budget dispute with his producers and wanted to know how quickly I could complete my scripting chores. Although, I'd already finished it I asked for two days time and we arranged a meeting for then. For some odd reason I felt the need to stall, but it seemed some relationships were unavoidable.

With that line of thought I'd began encouraging Antoinette to forge friendships with some of the neighborhood girls, they could be used for excuses and alibis. Susie is having a birthday party, Britney a sleepover, and the like. How quickly I found myself turning crooked, it was made easier by my very willing accomplice.

Chapter Nine

I was laying in bed waiting for Antoinette to return from a trip to the kitchen, she'd gone for a glass of ice water. I listened to the sound of the oscillating fan I kept on top of a chest of drawers. It'd been a noise I'd always found reassuring. Antoinette returned, other females I'd known would've slipped on a robe in a false front of modesty, she made no effort to conceal her nakedness.

Antoinette climbed into bed and offered me the glass in which she'd placed a straw. After I'd taken a drink she took some for herself and placed the glass on the night table.

'I forgot to brush my teeth,' she declared before she leapt out of bed and walked briskly to the connecting bathroom.

I got up and followed. I'd wanted to watch this bit of business. Antoinette stood over the sink dutifully going about with her orange toothbrush. Many mornings I had been brought to a smile seeing it resting in its holder. She rinsed, spat and wiped her mouth with her hand. I could never make another person understand the joy I derived from watching her perform these benign rituals. Finished, she turned to me, raised herself on tip toes and kissed me on the lips. I tasted peppermint.

We returned to bed, Antoinette rested her chin on my chest and trailed circles on my stomach with her fingertip.

'It looks like I've made some pals,' she informed me before she rolled over on her back.

'What are the names of these newfound companions?'

'Tara and Ruth Derbyfield, they live in a yellow house around the corner.'

We simultaneously turned on our sides so we faced each other.

'Are they nice girls?'

'Ruth is, but Tara seems a tad snobby.'

'That's how it often is with sisters, one sweet, the other sour.'

'I suppose so.'

Antoinette's brow creased as if she'd just remembered something. 'I need to wan you, my aunt is planning on inviting you over for dinner. I let slip that you were a writer. She loves playing patron to the arts. Plus, she's got this snooty friend who claims to be a fan of Salo and has been pestering my aunt to introduce you to her.'

The idea of dinner with Antoinette's aunt piqued my curiosity just slightly.

'What's the name of this friend of your aunts?'

'Enez Sparrow.' Antoinette elongated the woman's name so it came out sounding 'Eeeenneezz'. 'Even though she hasn't met you she acts all gooey like she has some crush on you.'

I heard a trace of annoyance in her voice, she obviously did not like this Enez Sparrow. I leaned forward and kissed Antoinette's forehead. 'Did you inform Miss Sparrow that I'm taken?' She climbed on top of me and instantly the beast began to grown.

'And expose you as the corruptor of her friends sweet, little niece?'

'My love, you are sweet. But I'm the one who's been corrupted.'

This caused a fiendish grin to emerge. 'I know, it's my proudest achievement.'

She then proceeded to corrupt me further.

Part Two

JUNE

Chapter Ten

It'd been a tradition in the film industry that once a screenwriter had delivered his completed script and shooting commenced that said screenwriter would be completely froze out, barred from the set and any rewrites handled by someone else. Nothing would've made me happier. I'd been on sets and found it dreadfully dull. Unfortunately, Passolini had decided that I needed to be present all the time. With great reluctance I'd relented to his wishes. In gratitude he bestowed upon me the additional credit of executive producer. It sounded impressive, but there were ten other individuals with that same title.

I'd instantly come to regret my decision. Passolini would have me rewrite a scene only to reject my revisions and shoot the original version. He demanded additional character development, something fans of his films had no interest in so long as the movie contained the requisite amount of gore and female flesh.

The situation was made further irritating by the presence of Sophia Bertuluchi, the film's female lead. She was a woman with meager talent, but looked great on film. She'd apparently taken a shine to me; between camera set ups she'd plop herself down in the chair beside mine and alternate between casual flirting and blatant passes.

Sophia processed a certain jaded beauty and while every straight male on set would've gladly severed a limb to sleep with her I would never have stooped to bedding an actress, even if I hadn't had Antoinette in my life.

She'd begun acting after she'd appeared in one of the higher end porn magazines, a fact she informed me of herself and one I was already aware of. It was her way of declaring her desirability and that I should want her. I'd contemplated lying, telling her I was homosexual. But I didn't think she'd have believed me. Besides, fibs like that tended to backfire and make women like Sophia even more persistent. Passolini had observed all this with great amusement. When lunch was finally called Sophia sulked to her trailer, she was known to have a cocaine habit and no doubt indulged once the door was shut. After she'd disappeared Passolini strode over.

'Matthew, I'm confused. Sophia makes every man here hard as a block of oak, but you react to her as if she's one of those pallid, child laden cows one sees inside supermarkets.'

A shrug of the shoulders was all I offered as a response.

His eyes went to slits. 'Oh, but of course, you're in love. When do I get to meet the little nymph?'

My body stiffened. 'That's an odd choice of phrase.'

He grinned broadly, 'Just an expression my dear scribe.'

We continued to stare at each other for several seconds, something about the look in his eyes I found troublesome when I informed him I was leaving for the day and he didn't protest. But as I walked away I felt his gaze on my back.

Chapter Eleven

That evening, in a move equally brazen and foolish, I'd decided to take Antoinette out to dinner. I don't know what inspired my decision; it hadn't been Antoinette, she'd made it clear that she'd been perfectly contented with our days and nights as they were.

Of course, we conducted our outing discretely. I'd chosen Milton's, a modest, but comfortable diner located two counties away where the chances of running into a friend or acquaintance would be slim. But in the unlikely event this occurred we'd agreed I'd introduce Antoinette as my cousin visiting from another state.

Antoinette gave her cut offs a respite and wore a short skirt of pale yellow with a matching blouse, it was a color that accented her tan and she'd earlier remarked on how she disliked wearing pants of any kind. She seemed to have sensed a playful role she could play in our little intrigue. As we sat across from each other the little devil would slide a foot out of its sandle and begin rubbing my leg. Ever so slowly she would work it upward until I was in such a state that standing was out of the question. My Antoinette wasn't the type of girl who said prayers before bed.

Once or twice I thought we'd drawn a questionable look prompted by Antoinette's low giggles, but they disappeared when confronted. I'd always relied on the cowardice of my fellow man. It was during dessert that I'd taken notice of a man, dining alone and who'd directed his gaze toward us. He was olive skinned with thick black hair and a mustache. He didn't turn away when my eyes met his. I didn't discern any disapproval, his face had remained quite blank.

I didn't bring him to Antoinette's attention and she'd taken no notice. He left before us and I didn't see him once we exited and walked to my car. What had troubled me was that he seemed vaguely familiar. I wondered if he could've been a member of the film crew, there were many whose names I didn't know. I quickly buried my worry, my cover story was solid and Sophia's antics was still the dominant topic amongst the set gossips.

After we'd returned home Antoinette treated me to a performance. I wouldn't grasp its meaning until much later, when all I had for company was my own thoughts.

One of the many things I'd inherited with the house was my father's cabinet stereo. It was an immense wooden monster, walnut, not that cheap fiber board. It'd been made at a time when hi fis were considered another piece of furniture and I felt the sound quality was much better than most newer models.

His extensive record collection had been included, it was made up mostly of vintage R & B, Rock 'n Roll, and lounge singers from the forties through the sixties. This accumulation of vinyl had been doted over like children, and my sister and I had been instructed on how to handle them. Antoinette and I ended up spending hours listening to them.

I'd seated myself in a chair and watched as she placed the Rolling Stones 'Flowers' album on the turntable and then gently placed the needle down on the track of choice. As the spinning notes of 'Ruby Tuesday' exited the speakers Antoinette began to dance.

Like legions of little girls she'd studied ballet. She'd accrued two years-worth of lessons until, in her words, puberty had arrived early and had made her too top heavy. She'd remembered many of the movements and was still very limber. I enjoyed this impromptu demonstration, simple yet elegant. But I'd failed to comprehend the message she was attempting to relay: that our time together, as it seemed then, was finite. We needed to live in the moment, happiness tended to be fleeting.

Chapter Twelve

I'd returned to Passolini's set, things were made somewhat bearable by the fact that Sophia had finally seemed to have accepted my utter indifference. She dealt with the rejection with an increase in her promiscuity, various crew members found themselves lured into her trailer or a convenient dark corner.

Later that afternoon shooting was halted when the film's leading man, a notorious drunk and hypochondriac, claimed a sudden bout of the flu. It hadn't been the first such instance. Passolini hadn't wanted to hire him in the first place. It'd been a concession to the man who held the purse strings. He was already behind schedule, so in an act of vindictiveness Passolini called it a day and sent everyone home.

He invited me to an early supper, I was initially hesitant, but there was something in his voice and face that told me it'd be unwise to refuse him. My mood lightened when we arrived at Siro's, the area's most exclusive eatery. In order to gain admittance one had to have membership, or be the guest of someone who did. There were only seven tables, six of which were indoors. Each only seated two and were placed so close together that one was always on the verge of jabbing their elbow into the side of the person sitting next to them. The establishment's exceptional food and wine list made the situation tolerable. The seventh and most desired table was located outdoors in the center of an enclosed courtyard. It allowed privacy and the opportunity for Passolini to enjoy one of his beloved Cuban cigars.

Over the course of our meal the conversation drifted between various topics from on-set gossip to his most current frustrations with his producers and then into a venomous tirade against a certain Sapphic film critic whom he held a particular disdain for.

'Nothing is more unpleasant than a lesbian forced to pay for her favors. I've also heard she's known to take lapses in her personal hygiene,' he said before exhaling a cloud of blue smoke. Passolini set the still-burning cigar in a heavy looking crystal ashtray, he crossed his legs resting his hands on raised knee. He then looked me straight in the eye and announce, 'I've been having you followed.'

I've never ran full speed into a brick wall, but that was the metaphor that instantly came to mind. After he'd waited a few beats for me to respond after my failure to do so, he continued, 'You see, after your confession of newly found endearment I became obsessed with discovering the girl's identity and you certainly weren't being very forthcoming.' He picked up his cigar and tapped off the excess ash.

'Now, you no doubt feel the need to express some display of indignation over my invasion of your privacy.'

Passolini brought the cigar to his mouth, he stoked it twice before exhaling another large plane of smoke. His blunt upfrontness had left me stunned. I felt like a child who'd been caught shoplifting. He took my continued silence as his cue to elaborate.

'You can't imagine my frustration. I didn't know you were such a homebody and your house is well camouflaged. So when the man I'd hired to monitor you kept reporting nothing of interest I'd decided to churn the waters by throwing that slut at you, but that proved to be an utter failure.'

I'd began to collect myself after recalling the lone diner from the previous night, but still wasn't clear on Passolini's motivations.

'I've enjoyed working for you, and wish to continue to. So, if this is some form of loyalty test …'

He interrupted. 'Matthew, please, it was simple curiosity, nothing more.'

'Then why not just ask?'

'My way was more entertaining, but I almost gave up. But last night my agent phoned me with the details of your outing. He did have trouble finding the words to describe your companion. I don't think there's a word for it in his native tongue. But I quickly realized what a ripe piece of fruit you'd plucked for yourself.'

'I'm not the one who did the plucking.' With my statement came Passolini's turn at silence as he quietly pondered my words. He leaned back in his chair. 'No, you've never struck me as the type to troll schoolyards. Just how did you meet?'

'I was working outdoors, I looked up and there she was, as if out of thin air.'

Passolini extinguished his cigar, he leaned in close, I instantly realized he was about to reveal a closely guarded confidence.

'I was once in the presence of one of these divine creatures. Long ago, I was fourteen and on holiday with my parents in Venice. Her name was Patia, she was also fourteen, the daughter of a local baker. Green eyes, with honey colored hair and an air of insolence. I was completely taken with her, would've slit my throat if she'd asked me to. But she found me barely worthy of nothing but a momentary glance.'

We were forced to pause our conversation while our table was cleared. After the waiter departed Passolini continued his divulging.

'We are artists, which makes us seekers of truth and professional liars. But it also makes us kindred, we both know that myths can, at times, transform into flesh. What Christians call transubstantiation, but in this case we're not talking about a Jewish carpenter. Instead, we refer to a female, of this world, but not, both sacred and profane. Tell me, what is her name?'

'Antoinette' came out like a sigh.

The sound of her name caused Passolini's eyes to take a melancholic cast, perhaps it was the resurfacing of memories of his beloved Patia who even after decades still had the power to enchant him. He reached into the inside pocket of his jacket and drew out a business card. He handed it to me, it was an action that seemed rehearsed. I accepted it and turned it over on its face. On a glossy black surface was written in guilded script:

The Bronze Peacock

In the bottom right hand corner was a phone number. I recognized the area code. It was local. Passolini refilled our wine glasses. 'It's an exclusive fraternal organization made up of men with the identical blessed curse as you. They're expecting your call.'

He took a drink and looked at me with a mixture of envy and sympathy. 'Imbibe from this cup as often as you can, one never knows.' His voice trailed off with his thoughts, I imagined back to Patia.

Later that night I watched Antoinette while she slept. She seemed at such peace; her face almost cherubic. I could've almost forgotten she was the same girl who'd engaged in the torrid activities only hours before.

I'd decided to hold off informing her of my conversation with Passolini. I was still absorbing it myself and felt further investigation was required. Antoinette let out a sleepy sigh and then turned on her side, draping one of her legs over mine. I wondered where I was headed and would there be anyone to catch me when I fell.

Chapter Thirteen

The following morning Passolini phoned to tell me I was no longer required on set, his investigation had concluded. Sophia was conducting an affair with the first assistant director, the leading man was receiving regular injections of vitamin B and all was right in the world.

Later that afternoon Antoinette's warning came to pass. I received a visit from her aunt. Christine Fairfield was the type of woman people used to call brassy. Her hair was dyed an unnatural shade of blonde and teased high, I saw grey at the roots. She'd no doubt cut quite a figure when young. Her body, at least covered by clothing, was still pleasantly formed. I could see where Antoinette had inherited her assets. But when Christine stepped from the shade and to the harsh rays of the sun her excessive use of make-up became apparent, a desperate attempt to conceal the consequences of time. She held her cigarette high, her breath smelled of gin, it was only quarter past noon. After she'd introduced herself we engaged in some inconsequential small talk before she finally got around to the reason for her visit and extended the invitation to dinner.

'Cocktails at six, dinner to be served at seven. Charlie, he's my gentlemen friend, just bought me a new grill, so we'll be dining outdoors on my deck.'

Despite the short notice, I accepted, curious to see Antoinette in the same setting with this woman. When she stepped off my front porch she'd looked over her shoulder and tossed me one of those expressions that some females never realize has long ago ceased being effective. I watched her walk away, her body moved with an exaggerated bounce.

Chapter Fourteen

I'd arrived at Christine's a few minutes early, she answered the door with a cigarette pinched between two fingers of her right hand, a half-filled tumbler in the other. When she leaned and planted a forward kiss on my cheek I caught the odor of bourbon mixed with her heavy perfume. She then took me by the arm and ushered me in, I was somewhat surprised by the tasteful décor. Given Christine's personality I'd expected animal prints and heavy shag carpet, instead I was greeted by muted pastels and wooden floors.

Introductions were made.

'That's my Charlie,' she said pointing to a sullen looking man sitting on the couch.

'Charlie Mattuna,' he muttered and nodded. It was obvious that Charlie was no gentleman. He had a prison yard body, his curly brown hair was closely cropped and his eyes devoid of empathy. His mouth curved in a subtle smirk that never completely disappeared.

I then met the third dinner guest. 'And that's Enez. My oldest and dearest.'

'Enez Sparrow,' she said as she extended her hand, I gripped it lightly, her skin felt cool.

Enez had maintained herself with greater care than our hostess. Her pale skin was flawless, she wore her copper colored hair in a short, precisely cut bob. But her most distinctive feature were her eyes, large, the color of jade. I'd only looked into them for a moment before I realized she was a cracked mirror.

After Christine had instructed me to sit, next to Enez, she briefly disappeared into the kitchen. During her absence I noted the walls covered with her photos, all looked to have been professionally taken. Over the course of that evening I learned that Christine had had a career in modeling. She'd been quite successful until a marriage stopped it cold. This husband was long dead, but he'd left Christine a generous inheritance that she was steadily drinking away.

When she returned several minutes later she was carrying a tray of gin and tonics, the gin had been heavily favored. I'd begun to wonder why Antoinette had so far failed to join us. Christine picked up on my confusion, 'Something the matter?' I took a drink before answering, 'I was just wondering where your niece was.'

Christine snuffed out her cigarette, 'Oh, I sent Antoinette over to the Derbyfield's for the night. I could tell she was a little miffed at being exiled, even if she didn't say so. But this evening is for adults only.'

Charlie had already finished his drink. 'I'm going to go put the meat on,' he said aloud to no one in particular before exiting the room.

As Christine lit a fresh cigarette, Enez asked, 'So, how has it been having Antoinette here?'

'She's been very good about staying out of my hair, not that I was ever worried, she's always been a well-mannered child. But I've developed a minor suspicion.'

A thin smile stirred across Enez's face, 'Really, do tell.'

Christine blew a smoke ring, 'It's nothing serious, I just believe she may have a little romance brewing. I'll respect her privacy, of course. I just pray her virginity stays intact.'

It was a struggle to keep a natural expression on my face, me being the one with the carnal knowledge. Fortunately, Enez changed the subject to Passolini's films. It turned out she really did seem to know his body of work and she peppered me with the usual questions. I fed both women some of the choice pieces of gossip, both devoured every scrap. I'd found most people enjoyed hearing about the dirty, little secrets of strangers.

At some point during the conversation Enez mentioned she was also in the entertainment business.

'Is that what you're calling it now?' remarked Christine. Enez didn't elaborate, nor did I ask her to. The congenial air was pierced by Charlie.

'The meat's ready,' he shouted.

We adjourned outside on Christine's wooden deck that looked out at her meticulously kept backyard. My second surprise of the evening came when Charlie displayed his one discernible skill, the man could actually cook a decent steak. Our conversation, lubricated by alcohol, flowed easily and thankfully remained superficial. Antoinette was never mentioned again, although I tried to imagine what she was doing. Did adolescent girls really engage in pillow fights?

After dinner Charlie and I were left alone while the women went inside to load the dishwasher. My offer to assist had been politely rebuffed. I was the guest, after all.

'I could use a beer or three, you want one?' Charlie asked. I nodded in the affirmation. While he was gone I sat somewhat dumbfounded by the fact that Antoinette shared lineage with Christine and had become curious to know what her mother was like. My musings were cut short by Charlie's return. He opened two bottles from a six pack and handed one to me. I supposed this was some feeble attempt on his part at male bonding. I'd decided to humor the situation, but before I could say a word he let out with, 'A little romance my ass.'

'Excuse me?' I uttered stupidly.

He took a pull from his beer. 'I overheard Christine when I was in the kitchen looking for the tongs. She's got this idiotic notion that that niece of hers is some sweet, little girl playing spin the bottle and holding hands with one of the local shits.'

'You think otherwise?'

'Jesus Christ, you've seen how she's built and Christine allows her to walk around the neighborhood half naked. Somebodies getting a taste of that pie.'

My mind went into a movie montage. Charlie strapped down on a table, me shoving a red hot poker down his throat, the sound of his wet flesh sizzling.

He hadn't finished. 'I'm telling you, God's a right son of a bitch tempting us like that. Well, so we can't touch, but we can still look.' He lifted his beer and winked.

My murder fantasy was forced to cease when Christine and Enez returned, both with drinks in hand. The remainder of the evening I spent listening to Christine regale us with stories of her glory days of modeling. I got the distinct impression I was the only one hearing them for the first time. I feigned interest and tried to ignore the vampish looks Enez tossed in my direction. I sensed tension coming from Charlie. At the time I attributed it to the excess attention I was being paid by both women. In a private moment before I left Enez invited me to her place for a night cap. I gently rebuffed her with an excuse of having an early morning. Later the thought of sex with Enez caused me to shutter.

I walked home drunk and felt profoundly exhausted. Charlie's remarks slow burned and Enez's pass reminded me why I'd acquired anti-social tendencies. I became overcome with an intense feeling of loneliness. I missed Antoinette. When I finally arrived home I went straight to my bedroom, stripped and fell into bed.

Despite my fatigue I couldn't fall asleep, instead I tossed and turned for almost an hour. My bedside phone rang; odd because I thought I'd disconnected it. For some reason I felt compelled to answer it. I picked up the receiver and put it to my ear.

'Matthew,' Antoinette whispered, 'having trouble sleeping?'

'Yes. I miss you.'

'Close your eyes and I'll give you the next best thing.'

Chapter Fifteen

That very night I had a dream, unlike any I've had before or since. I was never able to conjure specific imagery, only a series of sensations. I'd found myself being engulfed by sensuality, which pinned me down and fed off me. This intense feeling of desire finally burned me to a cinder. At no time was there any fear on my part, just a willingness to submit. I spent the final hours of that night sleeping like a contented child.

I awoke to stained sheets that smelled of sweat. My mouth felt dry, so I went downstairs to the kitchen. I kept a pitcher of ice water in the refrigerator. I didn't bother pouring some into a glass but instead drank from the container until I'd consumed half of the pitcher.

Later that day I found myself walking amongst the trees on the front yard, as I moved closer to the edge I'd begun to hear the rinky dink strains of a song. Once I'd made it to the foot of the driveway I finally recognized it as 'The Entertainer,' the calling card of the ice cream truck. As I looked down the block I could already see parents and children lining up.

I then spotted Antoinette, she was standing across the street. She wore a tube top, light violet in color and a matching skirt that hung low on her hips. Her ensemble appeared painted on. Her skin glowed and had turned a deep sable, her hair turned golden under the midday sun. I could almost understand Charlie's frustration, Antoinette left a trail of lust.

Just as I'd positioned myself directly across from her she became obscured from my view by the ice cream truck. She made her purchase from the driver, a white haired man in his sixties. At his age beholding a vision such as Antoinette could've proved fatal, but he managed to drive away.

Again she was visible to me and our eyes met. I became entranced as she brought the vanilla ice cream cone to her mouth, the pure white of the ice cream, the pink of her tongue as it emerged to taste it and then lick her glossy lips. Those same lips curled into a wicked smile while her free arm she held akimbo, and her left hip turned up. That was the moment our relationship solidified, she was master, I was her servant completely bound to her. It was the happiest moment of my life.

It was only upon reflection that the reality of the previous night came to me. It hadn't been a dream, but a visitation. Antoinette, my melodious demon lover had come to me, and while I'd been in my unconscious state she'd taken what she'd desired with the impudence of a tyrant. I was a slave in love with the knowledge of his bondage.

Chapter Sixteen

When I'd returned there was a message on my answering machine. At first I thought it was from Passolini, but it turned out to be from the Sparrow woman. How she'd obtained my number, which was unlisted, was a mystery. She extended an invitation to join her for drinks, there was a note of false coyness in her voice that I found irritating. I realized I should've been more direct the previous evening. I knew that I'd eventually have to set Enez straight and I could have then, all I had needed to do was return her call. Instead I chose to procrastinate.

That night as Antoinette and I sat on the floor listening to records she informed me that Christine spent up to four nights at Charlie's and never returned home until after noon.

'The others she simply falls asleep on the couch. My poor auntie. Still, she lets me be so long as my room is kept clean and I show up for lunch. Today we had chicken salad sandwiches.'

I hadn't mentioned seeing her that afternoon, she didn't bring it up, either. There didn't seem a need to. I was afraid that if it was discussed out loud it would somehow lose its vividness. Instead I asked about her sleepover at the Derbyfields. She let out a sigh of annoyance. 'Tara and Ruth are so vile and stupid. All night they stuffed their faces with potato chips and talked about their classmates, who are people I don't know. It all seemed as repulsive as St. Joan of Arcs.'

'Is that where you go to school?' It seemed like an odd notion, Antoinette in school.

'Yep good ol' St. Joans. Maybe one day they'll burn me at the stake,' she let out in a burst of laughter.

It's suddenly occurred to me that it was a place she'd eventually return to.

'What's the matter? All of a sudden you look so glum,' she asked as she took hold of my hand.

'It's nothing, I was just trying to imagine how you looked in your school uniform. Do you wear cardigans or pullovers?'

'Cardigans, hunter green, one wood, one angora and one cashmere.' Antoinette then leaned in and whispered into my ear, 'Let's go to bed.'

Chapter Seventeen

I was awoken by an explosion of thunder and the sound of rain that pelted the roof. I'd looked over and saw that Antoinette was no longer lying beside me. Although I felt no panic I still decided to get out of bed and go search for her.

It hadn't taken long. I found her downstairs sitting in front of the sliding glass door that led out to the patio. Both of us had remained undressed as we watched the heavy drops of water splattering against the windows and tile floor of the patio. The house was sporadically illuminated by lightning flashes that allowed us to see the trees whipping in the wind.

After I'd sat beside her she'd first said nothing, she just leaned her head on my shoulder. Finally, after some time had passed Antoinette spoke, her voice hushed, 'I love thunderstorms, the elemental violence how it seems there's a danger of the world being torn in half like a scrap of paper.'

'Would you tell me about your family,' I'd asked spontaneously. Antoinette lifted her head and looked at me with a puzzled expression, which turned to a smile. 'You're a funny one.'

She shifted her body so she could lay on her back and place her head in my lap.

'Mom's the disciplinarian, and in my opinion, a bit overprotective, maybe it's because I'm an only child. My Dad, on the other hand, is a complete softie, my Mom's always telling him I'm going to end up spoiled.'

I began to wonder how well Antoinette's parent's really understood their child. I'd began to stroke her hair, shadow rain ran down the length of her body. 'What do they do for a living?'

'They're both professors at NYU and both writers, but obviously not like you. The books they write are bought by many, but finished by few. I've tried reading one or two of them, but they just fell out of my hands.'

'What are they about?'

'Economics of the third world. I told you about how they've dragged me along to visit some arm pit of the world, right now they're in Guatamala. Thank god, Aunt Christine was able to convince them to leave me behind this time. Personally, I think they only go to these places because they feel guilty.'

'Guilty, why should they feel guilty?'

'Because they're well-off, white Americans. They're always throwing these dinner parties, I munch cheese and crackers, and eavesdrop. Everyone's a total gossip: who's having an affair with a student, who's cheating on their spouse. It's a riot.'

'Sounds like one.'

'Or, they complain about what they call intellectual state of the country.

Antoinette sat up, 'Speaking of affairs, I'm certain Charlie and Enez are having one. That Charlie is such a bastard, acts sly, as if I can't tell he's checking me out. And Enez's supposed to be my aunt's best friend. The whole thing's like one of those stupid soap operas on TV.'

She emitted a mischievous giggle and hugged my neck. 'If only my parents could see the sordid environment they've deposited me into. Under the roof of a lush who's being two-timed by an imbecile and a snob. Then there's you, whatever would my Dad do if he found out about the two of us?'

'If he was any kind of man he'd kill me with his bare hands and then send you off to a boarding school run by nuns.'

Antoinette brought a hand to her forehead in a display of dramatics. 'My lover murdered by my enraged father and me left to weep over your grave. How disgustingly romantic.'

We shared a laugh, our lives had become, to a certain extent, ridiculous. We then kissed and watched the storm as it ran its course.

Chapter Eighteen

I'd retrieved the card Passolini had given me and sat staring at the gold letters that spelled out 'The Bronze Peacock.' He'd told me they'd be expecting my call, but who were they? A kinky version of the Skull and Bones, a man-girl love organization? As it stood there were already two outsiders who knew about my relationship with Antoinette and it'd occurred to me that that was two people too many. I should've questioned Passolini further, but his disclosure of clandestine activity had set me off balance.

But as often is the case was my curiosity had begun to override my commone sense. I soon found the phone receiver in one hand, the other dialing the number. I felt the apprehension one feels when you don't have any idea what you're entering into. It rang three times before being answered, the voice on the other end was male, his tone agreeable.

'Executive services how may we help you?'

'My name is Matthew Dante, I was referred to you by Passolini Salo.'

A few moments passed, I heard the sound of papers being shuffled.

The voice spoke, it had brightened, 'Mr. Dante, of course, we've been expecting your call. You're very fortunate to have such a reference. Mr. Salo is an old and trusted friend. Is it your desire to apply for membership?'

'Yes.' I said it without thinking.

'Very good, but first there are some formalities. All applicants must submit to a complete background check. It's a matter of security. I'm sure you understand.'

'Yes, of course.'

'Once you've been checked, we'd like you to come down for an interview, very informal, consider it a friendly chat amongst friends. Fortunately for you there's a branch office in town. Now, if you don't mind, we're going to put you on hold briefly while we check our appointment schedule.' His voice was replaced with an instrumental version of 'Greensleeves.' Aside from his constant reference to himself in the plural our conversation had been normal. About twenty seconds passed before the voice returned.

'Thank you for waiting Mr. Dante. We have an opening this Friday at noon, would that be convenient?'

'Yes, I don't believe I've any pressing business.'

He proceeded to give me an address, it was in a part of town I was familiar with. Before our conversation was concluded there came a request.

'One final thing Mr. Dante, would you please bring us a photo?'

'A photo?'

'Of the young lady. We mean no offense, we're sure she's quite lovely, but we have a strict criteria.'

'I understand.'

'Very good. Friday, twelve sharp. Please call us if your day changes. We're looking forward to meeting you Mr. Dante. Have a pleasant day.'

After I'd set the phone down I noticed my hands were shaking. I poured myself a whiskey and after it'd sufficiently calmed me I realized I didn't have a single photograph of Antoinette, I should've possessed thousands. It was a situation I'd intended to rectify.

Chapter Nineteen

Fortunately, my photography equipment had returned with me from Europe. It only took a few hours to construct a dark room in the basement. Antoinette became visibly excited when I asked if she'd model for me. I was playfully chided for not requesting earlier. I hadn't yet told her of the reason for the session.

While I was setting up my camera Antoinette asked for a glass of wine, it had been the first time she'd requested alcohol and upon seeing my reaction she cocked her head and smiled.

'Really, Matthew, considering all the other acts we've committed together, over and over again.'

I couldn't argue, providing alcohol would've been the least of my transgressions.

'Pour yourself a glass and I'll put some music on.'

As I filled our glasses I heard the opening notes of 'Season of the Witch.' When I came back into the room Antoinette stood in front of the stereo, eyes closed, her body swaying to the music. She opened her eyes and I handed her the glass of red.

'To our dangerous union,' she said before she tapped her glass against mine.

We'd quickly finished our first glass so I retrieved the bottle. As Donovan's greatest hits continued to spin we began. Antoinette proved to be a natural in front of the camera, she effortlessly moved from pose to pose without instruction. She had taken her blouse and knotted it into a half shirt, along with her cut offs she managed to portray a kind of perversion of innocence. It was an ensemble that inspired a million fantasies of hitch hikers and farmer's daughters. All Antoinette needed was a country drawl and a piece of straw between her lips.

After three quarters of an hour I was satisfied I had more than enough, but Antoinette wished to continue. I watched as she shed her garments to reveal a matching pair of leopard spotted bra and panties.

I looked upon her body with a pronounced craving as she bared her shadow self, it'd been the reaction she'd desired. I brought the camera to my eye and we continued with our play.

Something sinister was brought out between us later that night. We clawed and bit each other's flesh, pulled each other's hair. Antoinette whispered in my ear between clenched teeth, asked to be called the most vile of names and when I'd comply we'd coil together tighter. When there was no place else to go we finally collapsed into satisfied exhaustion.

My face was buried in a pillow, both of us breathing heavily.

'Matthew, look at me.'

I lifted my head and was met by Antoinette's serene eyes. She'd allowed me a glimpse into the dark side of her sexuality. Her expression changed. It was something I didn't completely fathom. I saw a sense of pity, but also satisfaction. My teacher had instructed her pupil, I had to decipher its meaning myself.

Chapter Twenty

The day before my appointment I'd decided to tell Antoinette all after she'd remarked on how I'd seemed preoccupied. I showed her the card Passolini had given me, told her of his spying and my meeting the next day. I had to admit to her that I was still quite ignorant about the nature of the organization. I'd expected her to be at least a little upset over my withholding of information. Instead she took it all in calmly and seemed quite intrigued.

Antoinette placed herself in my lap and fixed upon me a look of gentle concern. 'This Passolini, do you trust him despite his habit of snooping?'

'As much as I'm capable of trusting someone other than you. Other than that original disclosure we've not come up in conversation. I think he's happy we've found each other.'

She'd been nodding slightly, something seemed to be turning in her mind, a subject she was reluctant to bring up, but had to.

'He isn't the one I was worried about, but Enez …'

Since leaving that phone message I hadn't thought of her, and had never bothered to return her call.

'Has something happened?'

'She's been asking my aunt and I a lot of questions. Aunt Christine hasn't picked up on it, but she's digging for something. When she speaks to me she condescends, thinks just because she's older it makes her smarter.'

Antoinette tucked her head under my chin in a rare display of vulnerability. 'Enez is fixated on you. She's spiteful and a grievance collector. I'm afraid she's going to try and hurt you somehow.'

I sroked her hair and kissed her brow in my best attempt to reassure her. 'You shouldn't worry. I've dealt with her type before.'

Antoinette snuggled up, she wanted to be held. I tightened my embrace. I believed I'd managed to relieve her worries, my own I wasn't so sure.

Chapter Twenty One

The following day I drove into the town's historic district where the tallest building, a bank, was a mere three stories tall. It'd been constructed in the nineteen twenties, a pale concrete monolith with a pair of cornices at the entrance. I enjoyed visiting this section of town, it's remained free of chain stores and second rate take-out restaurants. After finding a parking space across from the Italian bakery, still family-owned three generations deep. I grabbed an early lunch at Fred's diner. I'd felt a touch of anxiety and the food had helped settle my stomach.

The address I'd been given was a four block walk from the diner and as I made my way up the street I was again concerned over the possibility that I might cross paths with someone I knew. I'd completely ceased contact with my friends, ignored their numerous phone calls. What they'd thought of my continuous snubs I didn't know nor care. Even my relationship with Passolini had abated; Antoinette had become the center of my private universe.

When I arrived at my destination I found it was a single story, brown brick building. There was no signage save for a small bronze plaque that displayed the four numbers of its address. I counted three windows, all with thick shades drawn. I then noticed the intercom on the left side of the door. I pressed the button, seconds later the tiny speaker emitted a crisp voice.

'Good afternoon Mr. Dante, you're right on time. We appreciate that.'

It was followed by a buzzing noise. I reached down, turned the handle and let myself in. I stepped into a tiny foyer that was devoid of furniture or décor. A ceiling lamp illuminated the dark wood walls and a floor of egg white ceramic tiles. Directly in front of me were a pair of doors made of the same somber colored wood as the walls, each had an ornate gold handle that, because of their shape, reminded me of the feminine.

I'd only been standing there a few moments when the doors opened. A man emerged, he appeared 10 or so years older than I. He was dressed in a light grey suit, I could tell the way it fit him it had been tailored, his black shoes were twin mirrors. When I looked at his face I saw his dark hair was combed back, his steel grey eyes were vibrant, his teeth capped.

He smiled as he strode toward me, hand extended, silver cuff links winking. His grip was comfortably firm.

'Greetings, Mr. Dante. I'm Carpenter Gordon, we spoke on the phone. We trust you didn't have any trouble locating us.'

It was the use of the plural again. Despite all of the stillness around me I felt a pressure, an invisible other standing in the foyer with us.

'No, not at all,' I replied and he released my hand.

'Shall we?' he said motioning towards the opened doorway.

Carpenter closed the doors behind us. Before me was a hallway filled with what looked like six small offices, three on each side.

'We'll use the second suite on the left.'

I was let into a room finished with only a desk and two chairs. The furniture was antique, from the Victorian period. Mounted on the wall behind the desk was an enormous painting. It depicted a girl of Antoinette's age, almost as beautiful but with raven hair and porcelain skin.

'I see you've noticed Snow White,' Carpenter's voice broke my minor trance. 'Arresting, isn't it? I've had the pleasure of meeting the girl who modeled for the artist. He's a member, the painting a gift. Please have a seat Mr. Dante.'

After we'd each taken a chair I'd remained transfixed by the painting, the girl's blue green eyes seemed to look into me.

'We understand you're a screenwriter by trade, spinning frightful yarns for Mr. Salo's camera,' He'd said as a gentle prodding. I felt slightly embarrassed for being so easily distracted.

'Oh yes, not long, only been doing it for a few months.'

Carpenter's tone changed becoming slightly formal, but still friendly, 'Passolini is one of our more colorful supporters. Now, as we mentioned during our phone conversation we performed a background check. In your case it was just a formality, Mr. Salo having vouched for your character. Also, your last name seemed familiar. We looked into this and believe we'd met your late father.'

Since I'd entered the building I'd felt somehow off balance, but couldn't determine if it was intentional.

'Really, where exactly?' I said attempting not to sound suspicious.

'Oh, just through business contacts. He wasn't aware of our organization. You've our condolences, such a pity to lose loved ones. We understand you were particularly close with your sister.'

I heard screaming in my head and had to fight the urge to bolt. Carpenter's face softened, his eyes looked down at the desktop.

'We apologize, it wasn't our intention to dredge up painful memories. Let us change the subject.'

Carpenter gave me a brief history of the organization. It'd been founded in the mid-nineteen twenties by a successful silent film actor whose name I'd immediately recognized. The Bronze Peacock had been the nickname of his 13-year-old Polynesian lover who owned an extensive collection of feather boas.

Carpenter had reached into his breast pocket and had taken out a pair of gold-framed glasses, which he slipped on his face.

'Now, we'd like to see a photograph of your young lady friend. You did remember to bring one?'

'Oh yes, several actually,' I said as I reached inside my own coat and produced a small manila envelope.

Carpenter pressed his palms together, 'Take your time, select the one that you feel captures her best.'

I'd brought with me ten photographs, I carefully reviewed each. I hadn't brought any from the second set, those were for my eyes only. Finally, I selected a shot of Antoinette, in it she was seated in a chair, leaning slightly forward and looking into the camera with a lascivious expression. I momentarily flashed back to the evening it had been taken before I handed it over to Carpenter.

Before he looked at it he asked, 'May we ask where you had these developed?'

'In my dark room.'

'A photographer as well as a writer.'

He'd held the photo by the edges with his fingertips when he finally directed his eyes to Antoinette's image. I'd instantly noticed its effect on him. Carpenter seemed paralyzed, as if a strong electrical current was running through him.

'What is her name?' he whispered.

'Antoinette,' my voice was equally quiet.

Carpenter continued to gaze at the photograph. I'd become curious as to what he was thinking, was it possible he could see something that I couldn't? He finally handed the picture back and began tapping his lower lip with his right forefinger. I didn't know if this was a nervous tic of some kind, or if he was merely searching his mind for the proper words.

'Matthew, have you any idea how fortunate you are? He asked.

'Yes. She is of this world, but not.'

My response made Carpenter smile, 'We've been blessed, some may say cursed by the sight of many special females. But Antoinette is quite exceptional. I can imagine that it must be rather intoxicating to be in her presence.'

'She is both angel and demon. I believe she has many secrets, most of which I do not yet know. With each passing day it becomes increasingly difficult to imagine life without her.'

While I was speaking Carpenter had removed his glasses and had begun to clean them with a monogrammed handkerchief, but his eyes had stayed on me.

'Now you find yourself in a world where the very one who gives you rapture may also bring about your destruction. That is the sorrow of our wisdom and we welcome damnation with open arms.'

We'd come to a mutual understanding. We were worshippers of the girl child, the nymphet whose caress hurt as it lulled. Carpenter explained the group's rules. The most important was discretion, without it the secret would be out. The general public would never know of the organization's existence, extreme measure would be taken if necessary. There were certain members who held high positions in business, law enforcement and government, who would lend aid if possible. I didn't ask questions, I sensed I was under a period of probation, further information when I gained complete trust. Finally, Carpenter brought up the matter of membership dues, paid every six months. I informed him it wouldn't be a problem. Fortunately, I'd brought my check book. Carpenter told me to make it out to Executive Services. Our business completed he began to tell me of an upcoming event.

'Two weeks from today we're holding a coronation ball, it's one of our formal ceremonies and we only observe a very few every year. We're already set to crown two young ladies, if you and Antoinette are able to attend it will become a trio and its been years since we've had one of those.'

I was intrigued. I was sure Antoinette would be as well.

'We'll be looking forward to it,' I said.

'We understand this doesn't give you much time to prepare, so if there is any assistance needed please don't hesitate to call.'

'Thank you, I'm sure I can manage.'

'You appear more than capable.'

I suddenly felt the need to address the remark he'd made earlier. 'What did you mean when you understood my sister and I were extremely close?'

'I don't believe I used that word.'

'Still I found it an odd comment.'

'Then perhaps I should clarify. Your father was a casual acquaintance, and as I stated he wasn't aware of us. We once overheard talk of the lack of children in your neighborhood, how you and your sister relied on each other for companionship. Naturally we assumed your bond would be stronger than usual.'

His expression gave me some relief, 'Yes, we were often mistaken for twins.'

'We apologize for any offense given.'

Our meeting concluded with a handshake and Carpenter escorted me to the door. Once outside I was overcome by a feeling of lightheadedness. I was convinced the entire meeting had been monitored. I absent-mindedly put my left hand in my coat pocket and had felt a small object. I brought it out, it resembled a tiny bird cage with something stuffed inside. As I examined it closer I detected a faint odor, like some kind of herb. Puzzled, I placed it back in my pocket and promptly forgot about it. It wasn't until months later that I remembered the little charm.

Before returning home I stopped at a corner bar for a drink. While I sipped my draft memories of Alison crept in, how one summer she'd discovered a small clearing within the woods. It measured only eight by 12 feet, still we'd managed to construct a kind of fort where we settled our curiosities. During my first week home I'd tried to relocate it but had been unsuccessful.

But it felt unhealthy to dwell on the memory of my sister so I turned to eavesdropping on the conversations of the retired men who patronized the bar. They talked mostly about local politics and the baseball game that was on the television. Being in their twilight years their dreams had come to an end, but so had the burden those dreams carry.

Chapter Twenty Two

That evening I attended the wrap party for Passolini's film. It was yet another unavoidable obligation. I'd promised Antoinette I wouldn't be staying long. She already knew of the spare key hidden in the rock garden and was free to come and go as she pleased in my absence.

Within minutes of my arrival Passolini found me and had led me to a quiet corner of the room. Apparently, there was a female journalist looking for me, when he pointed her out and I saw that copper colored bob I instantly recognized Enez.

I told him of our acquaintance and that I could handle the situation. 'But don't be offended if I leave without saying goodbye.'

'Of course not, would you like me to have her ejected?'

I steered him away from the idea, why risk a scene. I reminded him that parties always come with their share of gadflys. We parted and I made my way to the bar, ordered a double vodka and after I downed half I approached Enez. Everything one needed to know about a woman like her could be found in her choice of footwear: knee-high black leather boots with stiletto heels. They'd no doubt left their imprint on more than one man's chest.

I'd met more than one Enez in my life. It all had its origins in father, she'd either received the wrong kind of attention, or none at all. Her life was spent in a search for a replacement that she wanted to love and destroy, and every man she encountered was seen as a potential candidate. When she saw me her eyes flashed. 'Matthew, I've a bone to pick with you,' she said in her school teacher tone.

I apologized with the explanation I'd been too busy to socialize. She smiled, it was like a surgeon's incision, 'So, who's the lucky girl?'

Her question caught me off guard and my face must have betrayed me because Enez emitted a laugh of barely concealed mockery.

'Lighten up, Matthew, that was a joke. I've heard about what a taskmaster Passolini's been. Probably already has you working on his next film.'

I lied and told her she was correct. She then took a step toward me, just close enough to be uncomfortable. When she continued speaking there was a slight shift in the sound of her voice.

'I was over at Christina's the other day, seems her niece is still in a huff over being left out of our dinner party. You know Matthew, I believe she has a little crush on you, it's really very cute.'

I knew Enez was lying, but couldn't grasp why. Antoinette didn't have 'huffs' and would never express a strong emotion toward me in front of her aunt, and definitely not in Enez's presence. I put on a front of ignorance, 'Antoinette's a sweet girl, if she's harboring some minor infatuation towards me I hadn't noticed and I'm sure it will pass.'

Enez rolled her eyes, 'Men, you never notice such subtleties. But you're probably right, eventually she'll forget all about you and aim her sights on someone her own age.'

In that moment I wanted to wrap my hands around Enez's throat and choke the life out of her. Had we been alone, I would've. But our conversation was interrupted by a man with an eastern European accent. Enez must have known him for she let out a squeal and hugged him. I took the opportunity to leave.

Later, after I returned home, I reported my encounter with Enez to Antoinette. She emitted a grunt of disgust. 'I can't stand her, always got her nose in the air like she's Queen Victoria. She's descended from a family of pig farmers for god's sake. And she's definitely fooling around with that stupid lug Charlie.'

I didn't realize it at the time, but my troubles with Enez had just begun. That night my only concern was Antoinette's and my mutual gratification. In that we were repeatedly successful.

Chapter Twenty Three

I'd just finished a phone conversation with Carpenter, he'd called to remind me about the coronation ball, which was still a week away. He'd also requested Antoinette's measurrements, favorite colors and shoe size.

'We thought we'd send some gowns over for her to try on.'

I'd already committed Antoinette's dimensions to memory and had been planning on taking her on a shopping spree. But Carpenter convinced me his was the safer route.

'Why attract unwanted attention?' he'd said.

When I'd first told Antoinette about the ball she'd agreed to go and had seemed mildly excited, but hadn't mentioned it since. My little Antoinette was a precocious girl and little by little she was revealing just how different she was compared to her peers.

She possessed a level of sensuality one didn't normally find in girls her age. She was aware of it and used it to arouse in me a feverish desire. I'd been unable to refuse her or her sinful requests.

Other things I'd learned about my adolescent love: She didn't daydream about pop idols or movie stars; She took some pride in her appearance, but didn't fuss about it; She was even tempered and not given to sudden mood changes. Although she occasionally took some joy in teasing me, it was always good natured, most of the time she used it as just another tool of seduction. Antoinette only seemed irritated after she'd spent time with little Ruth and Tara, her supposed friends.

'They were your idea,' she said, but I'd been forgiven.

I'd come to the conclusion that she didn't like to spend time with children her own age at all. She'd variously described them as immature, sloppy, obnoxious, boring, foul-smelling, and a dozen or so other adjectives. Our relationship had remained mostly sheltered, Antoinette had not complained or made demands, but I'd known she wished for an opening of barriers.

A few hours later when the gowns and shoes were delivered Antoinette displayed a howl of simple girlish delight. I'd opened a bottle of champagne and while seated took joy in watching her reaction with each box she opened. Antoinette would take a gown and disappear into the kitchen with it. A couple of minutes later she'd emerge and gaze at herself in the full-length mirror I'd set up for the occasion. She'd examine herself front, back and side-to-side, carefully inspecting how each dress fit the contours of her body.

Three of the boxes were never opened because she claimed she didn't like them. How she determined this sight unseen I didn't know.

'Female intuition,' was her response.

Finally, she selected a little black number with thin straps and plunging neckline. It'd also allowed her to display her bronzed legs.

'You know, I've had this body since I was eleven,' she said as she looked at herself in the mirror. It was said without a trace of vanity.

'It's probably why my mother is so over protective. I always thought she may have been a little jealous, she's rather flat chested.'

I've had this body since I was eleven. It played in a continuous loop inside my head. Had I encountered her at that age would I have been able to resist her? I dared not imagine. It was a question that scared me, and I was equally afraid of the answer.

Chapter Twenty Four

It'd been one of those lazy Sunday afternoons when a person found oneself idle. I hadn't yet received a new assignment from Passolini, nor had I seen or spoken to him since the wrap party.

Antoinette had gone, of all places, on a trip to the zoo with her aunt. The outing had been Christine's idea.

'She calls it family time,' Antoinette had informed me.

She felt she needed to humor her aunt whenever one of these excursions was proposed. Previously, they'd attended several movies; an outdoor rock concert, I couldn't recall the band's name; and a fashion show held in the local shopping mall. It was at that particular function that Christine had attempted to implant the idea that Antoinette should follow in her footsteps, a sort of passing of the torch. She played along without offering a firm commitment.

With my own lack of activity I'd taken to sitting on the patio and quietly sipping one beer after another. It was good every once in a while to get slightly inebriated after lunch. I was happy in my temporary solitude, it'd given me a chance to think. I'd been somewhat troubled that Carpenter had been acquainted with my father even if it had only been in passing. It reminded me that the man had largely been a stranger to me. But now that he was no longer among the living I felt it was better to leave that mystery unsolved.

Even while in that alcohol induced cloud a realization had become clear to me. I still had a chance to turn back, sever my ties with my home, Passolini and even with the Bronze Peacock. I could've pulled up stakes and gone to any place of my choosing, construct an entirely new existence. But even as those thoughts had been running through my mind I'd know I'd never exercise that option. I'd allow the window to close becaue I'd never be able to let go of Antoinette.

She possessed me, it was that simple and that complicated. It was unsaid and done without force, yet this 15-year-old girl had accomplished what so many others had tried and failed, with guile so subtle it was almost invisible.

From the very moment I'd encountered Antoinette the world around me had begun to shift, my perspective altered. Little by little it'd revealed a side I'd not known of. Of course, it had always been right in front of me, hiding in plain sight. Once seen it could not be unseen.

We have so few years of innocence, or is it blissful ignorance, before the poison finds its way and seeps into our system, and we become the walking damned.

Chapter Twenty Five

When the night of the coronation ball finally arrived I seemed to view it through the same hazy glow that had once accompanied Christmas Eve, like when I was a child and the world hadn't yet revealed its true face to me.

Antoinette and I had barely spoken as we prepared for the evening, but I silently marveled at the way her dress clung so perfectly against her body and at the ease she wore it. She'd just finished helping me with my tie when the headlights of a car swept across the front of the house. Carpenter had arranged a driver for us, I looked out the windows and saw the black Bentley idling, our chauffeur had already exited the car and stood waiting.

As we walked towards the front door I took the time to appreciate how the high heels Antoinette wore accentuated her legs. I'd become so used to seeing her in bare feet, so the sight of her in formal footwear was quite the novelty.

Once we were on the front porch I took Antoinette gently by the arm, guiding her down the steps and to the car. Our driver was a middle-aged man with olive skin dressed in a black uniform and cap, he offered us a slight bow as he opened the door for us.

Once we were on our way Antoinette pressed her body close to mine and we both stared out the window at the street lights, neon signs and stray figures as they blurred, leaving contrails of color and shadow.

We remained silent as civilization was replaced by primordial country. The moon, full and yellow like a cat's was hung above the spider web silhouettes of trees.

'We shall be there in a few minutes,' our driver quietly stated, the only words he spoke that entire evening.

He then made a left turn onto a road that had been invisible to me, the outside world seemed to have been doused with indigo ink. I gathered that he must have taken this route so many times that it had long been committed to his memory. The road was tree lined and occasionally curved, how long we traveled on it I don't know. But eventually I began to see a faint glow in the distance. I looked down at Antoinette as she held onto my arm, her cheek pressed against my shoulder. She smiled, a girl in the midst of an adventure.

When the road opened up we were greeted by the sight of a large estate, resplendent in an old world fashion. Even at that moment I wondered if we'd somehow crossed over onto an alternate plane. It rested atop a hill, which gave it the appearance of floating, its multitude of windows radiated a golden light that was soft and inviting. Its circular, cobblestone driveway was lined with vintage limousines similar to the one we rode in.

Antoinette had leaned forward to take in the sight, she'd cupped my hand in hers and I felt my pulse quicken as a child-like giddiness rippled through me. The car came to a stop at the home's front entrance, a uniformed valet stepped forward and opened the door. He then offered his gloved hand to Antoinette as she stepped out of the automobile.

'Good evening and welcome,' he said with a bow identical to our driver's.

I again took Antoinette by the arm as we ascended the steps, the valet walked slightly ahead, which allowed him to open one of the twin doors. We crossed the threshold and into an immense foyer where we saw the first of many crystal chandeliers, the size of a small car, I could only imagine how long it took to clean something so large and intricate. I heard music, but was unsure of where it emanated from. The air was thick with the fragrance of flowers that were gathered in elaborate bouquets that spilled from Chinese vases that stood five feet high.

We walked from the foyer into a large, circular room, a trident of halls splintered off left, center and right. Hung on the walls were a series of paintings, all were of young girls and appeared to be the work of the same artist who had been responsible for the picture in Carpenter's office. At the foot of each hallway were statues, also of young girls, but these each had a pair of gossamer wings sprouting from their backs. It felt as if I was viewing everything through a layer of gauze.

Suddenly, there appeared a girl, a Louise Brooks in miniature, the same age as Antoinette. She wore a silver, ankle-length gown that was slit on the side, a half-full champagne flute in her tiny hand. She stepped to us.

'Hello new faces, I'm Valerie.'

'I'm Antoinette, and this is Matthew.'

Valerie smiled slyly, both girls exchanged a look, I felt some secret had silently passed between them.

Valerie motioned with a slight nod of her head, 'Follow me, the others are gathered in the main hall.'

We followed her down the left side hall, the music growing louder as we walked. We finally came to the end of the hall and were confronted by a pair of ornately carved doors. Valerie, who appeared so diminutive never-the-less opened one as if it weighed nothing and the three of us walked into the house's main dining hall. The room was the size of a high school gymnasium. Hanging from its high ceiling were another pair of chandeliers as big as the one that hung in the foyer. They refracted jewels of light onto the polished wood fllor.

Small lamps were mounted along the walls, each had a trio of delicate bulbs that produced subtle illumination.

The music I'd heard earlier came from a twelve-piece orchestra seated on a riser that rested to the left of a stage at the opposite end of the room. Each musician was dressed in a white dinner jacket. But ther most unusual piece of attire was the eyeless mask each man wore on his face.

They played to an audience made up of men of various ages, all dressed in formal evening wear. All carried an air of wealth, some stood while others sat at round tables that were covered with white table cloths. At times one would pause to throw an admiring glance at one of the young girls who passed by on their way to the foot of the stage. There, about two dozen had gathered and were chatting amongst themselves and inspecting each other's gowns. Although they were all attractive none were as stunning as Antoinette. I watched as she silently took in her surroundings.

Carpenter emerged from behind a pillar, he looked lyrical in his tailored tuxedo and seemed to glide towards us. For the first time I found myself wondering what he did for a living. I'd managed to recognize some of the men in attendance. Many had had their pictures in the paper in either the business section or society column. All I knew had wives and children.

Carpenter wore a warm smile as he shook my hand, 'Matthew, so pleased you could attend.' He then turned to Antoinette and gently took her hand, 'You must be Antoinette.' I thought I heard a trace of awe in his voice.

She smiled. 'Pleased to meet you.'

'I see you've already met Valerie. Valerie would you be a dear and introduce Antoinette to the others?'

'Be happy to,' she took Antoinette by the arm and they went off towards the girls who were still gathered at the front of the stage.

A waiter appeared, a silver tray covered with champagne flutes balanced on white gloved hand. Carpenter plucked two and handed one to me. 'Matthew, perhaps you should take a moment to exhale.'

I had to grin over the remark, I'd been feeling overwhelmed by the deluge to my senses. My mouth had gone dry, the champagne burned cold as it went down.

'What you're feeling is to be expected, it was the same for me. That rush of emotions that comes with indulgence without consequence; to openly engage in what the outsiders consider perverse, or in the clergy's words – sinful.'

'I've never felt that way when I'm with Antoinette.'

Carpenter finished his drink and set the empty glass down on the nearest attendant's tray. He produced a gold cigarette case and offered one to me. I declined. After he'd lit up I smelled something mixed with the tobacco, possibly hashish.

'Of course you don't, nor should you. Your relationship with her has only recently fallen under the category of taboo. The people who've labeled it as such sexualize Antoinette while at the same time they infantize her. Mere decades ago a girl her age would have already been married off and fattened with her first child. These same enlightened guardians of virtue never consider that a girl as young as Antoinette could be the engineer of seduction.'

He waved his cigarette in the girl's direction, I saw Antoinette had already ingratiated herself to the others.

'Look at them, already as close as sisters, which spiritually they are.'

I redirected my gaze back towards Carpenter, his expression had turned introspective with a touch of melancholy.

'In a world filled with ugliness we dare to seek out beauty and embrace it. You're no doubt aware of what would happen if the two of you were discovered?'

'Yes, but I refuse to be caged.'

There was some false bravado in my pronouncement, when the notion of penalties raised its head I pushed it away. I'd decided not to tell Carpenter about Antoinette and my occasional dinners out. Carpenter's mood seemed to have brightened, he'd gotten a fresh glass and raised it high.

'Enough pondering, Hades is not yet on the horizon.'

I returned the toast and the both of us took a drink.

'Now, go to your Antoinette, revel in each other. Dinner will be served shortly.'

I required no further prodding. As I approached Antoinette I saw her having a conversation with a strawberry blonde. I saw they'd both removed their shoes which laid on the floor beside them, in fact all of the girls were barefoot. Upon seeing me Antoinette immediately entered my embrae and after bestowing a kiss on my lips she whispered in my ear, 'I'm so happy.'

As she should have been, she was with her own kind, perhaps for the first time. My chin brushed against her neck and I inhaled the scent of the pink bar of soap she used when bathing. Her skin felt softer than her dress's material. I felt myself surrendering to a minor fit of nympholepsy when the dinner bell rang.

I turned and found Carpenter standing behind me, Valerie was on his arm.

'We'd love it if the two of you would sit with us,' she said.

As Antoinette and I followed them I saw that the tables had already been set. I couldn't recall seeing this being done but assumed I'd been distracted by my conversation. Once at our tables each man joined in what seemed like a choreographed gesture, each held out their companions chair allowing the girls to be seated first. I followed suit, the ladies seemed to enjoy this simple act of gallantry.

After I'd sat myself down I'd taken a moment to appreciate how the light from above reflected off the dinner ware, and made it appear lustrous. While Antoinette had chosen not to wear any jewelry, many of the other girls wore diamonds or pearls that sparkled like drops of dew. There seemed to be a feeling of euphoria in the air.

The appetizers consisted of caviar topped deviled eggs and oysters. For an entrée, three choices were offered:

Chicken with braised leeks, spinach and apples.

Roast turkey with cranberry sauce, turnip puree, green peas and roasted potatoes.

Filet mignon lili with creamed carrots and chateau potatoes.

Both Antoinette and I chose the third option and she ate with her usual lusty appetite, as did all the girls, it was yet another thing they held in common.

There was a brief repose after dinner before everyone's attention was directed towards the front of the stage. There, a stout man was standing in front of a microphone. I guessed him to be in his late fifties or early sixties. He had a full head of silver hair and a mustache that had been waxed at the tips so the curled upwards like a pair of devil's horns. He wore a pink carnation in his lapel and clutched an ivory handled cane in his left hand. I saw a table had been set up on the floor beneath him, on it rested three gold wreaths.

I watched as everyone rose from their chairs and made their way towards the stage. I took Antoinette by the hand and followed. The man hadn't made any verbal announcement yet had somehow managed to bring the room into attention. He cleared his throat and began to speak in a light baritone.

'Ladies and gentlemen, let me take this opportunity to welcome you. My name, for those new to the proceedings, is Cuthbert Laroson and I've been bestowed the honor of master of ceremonies for the evening. For tonight we crown not one, but three maidens. I would like to call to the front of the stage Sasha, Keicho and Antoinette.'

There was a gentle round of applause as Valerie collected Antoinette and along with the other two took them to the appointed spot.

'The rest of you ladies form a circle.'

The remaining girls obeyed, they formed a circle around the ones at the foot of the stage and joined hands.

'Behold they who've been honored with song and verse, the return of Dionysus, Hermes, Pan and the hunter goddess Artemis. The myth mends flesh, the glorious nymphet.'

A sound arose, it'd started low but steadily grew in potency. I'd finally realized it was the girls who stood in the circle, they were chanting a series of names:

'Auraes, Astiriac, Hesperides, Aegle, Arethusa, Erytheia, Maia, Electra, Taygete, Celaino …

The man's face turned Heavanward, 'Divine ones, we who are at your mercy, lost without you. Please accept our love, for it is all we have to offer.'

'Lumahides, Naparac, Orodemniades, Anthousac, Dryadis, Daphnaiais, Kissiac, Melias, Hyleoroi …

Antoinette's eyes met mine, she behaved as if everything that was occurring was natural, expected and deserved.

…Crinaiar, Eleiouomac, Pigniar, Corytiar …

Without any prompting Valerie had begun to place a wreath on each girl's head. I felt the air had changed, there was an unseen but still palatable presence in the room. The man's voice had begun to tremble as he neared his conclusion.

'Our love may bring punishment, perhaps even perdition's flames, but our hearts will remain open to you. If you decide to cast us aside we ask for our final act of charity, a single kiss from your precious lips.'

As Valerie placed the wreath upon Antoinette's head I felt a tingle shoot up my spine. Every light in the room surged, then in the blink of an eye the world around us went black. A minor commotion followed consisting mostly of the girls' laughter. I'd chosen to remain quiet and didn't move from the spot I'd been standing in despite the multiple bumps against my shoulders and the apologies that followed.

Our time in the dark probably had lasted no more than 20 or 30 seconds before power was restored. The first thing I saw in front of me, Antoinette's poised and barefoot, so close I could've reached out and touched her. On her face she wore a devious grin that said, 'How naughty of me.'

The music resumed, Antoinette stepped to me. On tip toes she kissed me, it burned sweetly. IT was the last thing of that evening I can remember with complete clarity.

In the months that followed there were times I questioned the reality of that night. I was continuously reminded of the tale of the lone traveler, lured from the road and taken to the land of fairie, never to be seen again.

Chapter Twenty Six

I'd come to the decision that I should begin a thorough investigation of the record collection, separate the keepers from the ones I'd eventually get rid of. I began with the singles of which there were four cases. Fortunately, they'd been organized alphabetically.

While Annete Funicello was working her way through 'Pineapple Princess' I'd gone into the kitchen to grab a beer out of the refrigerator. I returned to the sight of Charlie, he was standing in front of the stereo staring down at the rotating disk as if hypnotized.

'Charlie,' I said, but he didn't budge.

'Charlie,' I shouted. That seemed to have rousted him for he turned to face me.

'What the hell kinda song was that?' he asked as he scratched his crotch.

'It was one of my father's records.'

For some reason that made him smirk. He took a half pint of vodka from the back pocket of his jeans, unscrewed the cap and took a drink. After he wiped his mouth on his arm, he asked, 'Have you seen Antoinette, has she been over here today?'

It was the last question I'd expected from him.

'No, I haven't. What would make you think she'd be here?'

He squinted then unsquinted his eyes, finally he stared up at the ceiling, 'Don't know, I guess you just seem like the type she'd enjoy pestering.' He leveled his gaze back to me. 'She didn't come home for lunch, heaven forbid she misses one of Christine's goddamn chicken salad sandwiches.'

I'd begun to feel uneasy, but knew if I allowed it to show it would only embolden Charlie. 'Well, as you can plainly see she's not here, but if I do see her I'll let her know her aunt is looking for her.'

Charlie took another drink, he turned slightly and I realized how drunk he really was.

'She's probably with her chippy, like she was last night.'

Another drink, the bottle was half empty. Against my better judgment I asked, 'What do you mean?'

'Last night after Christine and I had left the bar, we were going to head straight back to my place. All of a sudden she asks me to stop at her house, needed to pick up some damned thing or another. But when we get there she was out cold. Then I figured, I'm here, might as well have a peek, see how the little princess was doing. But when I looked in her room she wasn't there.'

'What did you tell Christine?'

My question took him slightly aback. 'I told her the kid was sawing logs. That girl's no kin to me, what do I care what kind of bullshit she's up to. And I waited until morning, wasn't about to spend the entire goddamn night looking for that brat.'

Charlie took a final gulp from the bottle before he shoved it back in his pocket. He sniffed loudly and fixed me with a quick look.

'You know there's something about you I haven't quite figured, Matthew.'

'I could say the same thing about you, Charlie.'

'Suppose so.'

Without another word he turned and let himself out the patio door. I kept a few steps back as I followed him. He made his way to the foot of the driveway where a car sat waiting. Charlie got in on the passenger side, but I was unable to see who was driving.

An hour later Antoinette was lying on her stomach in the middle of the room, legs bent at the knee as they swung up and down. She sipped a cherry Coke through a straw and was listening to Connie Francis.

She had greeted me with her usual affection, but without a word as to her whereabouts. I'd not asked her, instead I'd taken notice of the outfit she wore. It was a white half top with yellow, orange and black polka dots and a matching pair of shorts. She'd occasionally dressed this way, it made her appear even younger than she was. She'd go so far as to alter her hair style, like the addition of the white barrette that she wore. OF course this little girly girl look aroused me.

I sat down on the floor beside her, she pretended not to have noticed.

'Why do you feel the need to dress like this?'

She turned on her side and in her best baby doll voice said, 'To remind myself that before you started molesting me I was innocent and pure,' she paused, then when she was pleased by the reaction she elicited she spurt out a giggle.

When I brought up Charlie's visit and his discovery of her absence Antoinette simply bit her lower lip and rolled her eyes, 'He's had all sorts of lewd thoughts about me, but he'll never act on them. He wouldn't risk losing his sugar momma.'

'What if he decided to tell your aunt about your being gone in the middle of the night?'

'I'll just tell her the big drunk oaf went into the wrong bedroom.'

I remained silent, Antoinette sat up, 'Why are you so sulky today?'

I could only shrug, the next thing I know I was on my back and looking up at Antoinette as she'd peppered me with kisses.

'Don't let that Charlie bother you.'

'I won't.'

'Now, be honest, you like it when I dress like this.'

'I do.'

I felt her hand as it made its way to my groin.

'What do we have here?' her tone was one of lewd curiosity.

As she proceeded to perform on me in a most unholy of manner I closed my eyes and added another entry in my ledger of sins.

Chapter Twenty Seven

The following afternoon I had lunch with Passolini, he'd been attempting to contact me and I'd realized I'd have to somewhat satisfy his curiosity about the coronation ball. I shared the basic details, but omitted the odder aspects of that night. He seemed satisfied with this version of the event.

As was the norm our conversation turned to gossip, even when not in production we remained rumor traders. Apparently, Sophia's drug dependency had increased to the point of being almost lethal. Passolini speculated it was the result of the distress she felt after a recent abortion. I knew of at least three previous procedures.

'It was that first assistant director's,' he said through a cloud of cigar smoke. 'She'd fallen for him and wanted to have the child, but he pressured her to get rid of it, which she did.'

The idea of Sophia being acquainted with guilt was a notion I found hard to fathom.

'Well, she was raised Catholic after all,' Passolini offered.

When I'd returned home I'd instantly sensed something was off, I went from room to room, but at first I couldn't find any evidence to support this feeling. It was only when I made my way upstairs that I caught the scent – perfume – faint at first, but it grew stronger as I continued to ascend. One thing was certain the odor hadn't belonged to Antoinette. She was allergic to perfume, so much so it gave her headaches. The fact that the smell still hung so strongly in the air meant that the intruder had only recently departed.

When I relived the incident it was obvious who the trespasser had been. But at the time I'd been in a mild state of panic and not thinking clearly. My first concern was the security of my collection of Antoinette's photos. I found them undisturbed. I then examined all the house's doors and windows. Every one was locked, I felt confusion instead of relief.

I was standing in the kitchen when I felt a pair of hands on my shoulders, it caused me to jump like a startled animal. I spun around to find Antoinette staring at me with a look of puzzled amusement.

'Don't you ever make any noise when you walk?' I exclaimed.

'Nope.'

I took her into my arms and apologized. I'd decided not to tell her about the intruder. It didn't seem right to burden her with my misgivings.

Part Three
JULY

Chapter Twenty Eight

It was the fourth of July, I'd spent the better part of the day on the patio punching up a script for one of Passolini's friends. I'd come to regret the assignment, not that the work was difficult but because the whole notion of responsibility had become distasteful.

There were four beer bottles on the table, three empty, one full. It'd become a habit of having a few while I wrote. I'd paused for a moment to rub my eyes when I heard Antoinette's voice chirp.

'Howdy neighbor.'

Her hair was damp as was her white tee shirt, which made her bikini top visible. She took the towel that was wrapped around her neck and draped it over the chair closest to mine. After she'd sat down she kicked off her flip flops and launched into an account of her day.

'I was just at Danny Milligan's house, he's Ruth's grubby boyfriend,' she emphasized the word boyfriend with a slight tone of disgust, it was obvious she didn't care for this Danny.

'He has a pool in his backyard and I couldn't resist taking a dip. He spent most of the afternoon leering at Ruth and I, like he'd never seen a girl in a bathing suit. Boys his age are so obvious, just like boys your age.'

'Maybe I should have a pool installed,' I said before taking a sip of beer.

She motioned for me to pass her the bottle, which I did.

'Not a good idea, people might start to talk.'

She winked and took a drink. She set the bottle down, got up and started to stretch, her arms raised, back arched. Antoinette's tee shirt rose up and I got a peek at her flat, tanned stomach.

She then approached and leaned over me, bracing herself on the arms of my chair. She moved in closer until our foreheads were touching.

'Having fun?' I asked

'Of course I am.'

She began to slowly move her hips back and forth.

'I'm reading your mind Matthew and I must say you have some rather perverse ideas.'

This was one of her more wicked games and one we'd played before. The chief rule being that I wasn't allowed to touch her, all the while she'd tease me towards the cliff's edge. As she contined to press against me her voice became hushed, her breathing heavier, I felt its heat on my eyelashes.

'All those things you want to do to me. I've let you before, even though I know I shouldn't have. I just can't help it, I'm just a very bad little girl.'

It was only when I was on the verge of insanity that she took me inside and rewarded me with her favors. Afterward, she layed next to me.

'You must curse the day we met,' she said with glee.

Before I could respond she'd changed the subject.

'My aunt sent me over to invite you to join us at the park for the fireworks.'

'What time should I arrive?'

'A little before eight, and remember, there'll be a crowd, so you'll have to keep your hands to yourself.'

She let out another chuckle and proceeded to perform one more act of blasphemy. Yes, Antoinette was a very bad little girl. I'd wondered how she'd learned to do the things she did. Many times I was about to ask, only to think better of it. Instead I devised lurid fantasies involving a ring of nubile, robed girls standing before a raging fire. All around them a black forest. They'd let their robes drop revealing their naked bodies and one by one they'd receive instruction from satyr. My work on Passolini's films had had their influence on me. Antoinette's fervid moans brought me back to reality.

Chapter Twenty Nine

I'd left the house at dusk. Manner Park, where the fireworks were being held, was only three blocks away, I'd decided to make the journey on foot. The outside temperature had lowered to a comfortable seventy three degrees and there was a slight breeze that caused the tree leaves to gently rustle. While on my stroll I recently rehearsed my behavior for what would be the only time I'd spend with Antoinette while in the presence of her aunt. I really hadn't doubted my ability for restraint, Antoinette's warning had been nothing more than a jest.

Instead I found myself recalling the previous day's mystery, as well as Charlie's bizarre intrusion and Antoinette's belief that he was carrying on an affair with Enez.

'I'm afraid she's going to try and hurt you.'

Antoinette's words echoed in my head. Did the Sparrow woman hold some evidence of my illicit affair with Christina's charge. But try as I might I could not come up with any loose ends. I'd spent a fair share of my time on movie sets, places that were always rife with petty intrigues, might they have induced in me a subtle form of paranoia? Or was it possible I was feeling guilt over sleeping with a high school sophomore?

I'd allowed these thoughts to dispatch as I reached the entrance to Manner Park. The fireworks were well attended, there were cars parked bumper to bumper on both sides of the street. Clusters of people dotted the landscape, overtanned women who were dressed too young, their mates either sunburned or pale as ghosts. They mingled alongside the withered elderly and the sticky fingered children who dashed about burning off their soft drink-fueled rushes.

I hadn't attended the fireworks since I'd been a boy the same age as Antoinette. I'd fond memories of those occasions, when my parents seemed truly relaxed. I recalled a catalogue of little details, the smell of grilling hot dogs, the din of random laughter mixed with the music spilling from numerous radios, Alison in shorts, her sockless feet in a pair of Keds.

My eyes swept the crowd, but I failed to spot Antoinette. Then I felt her hand touch my elbow ever so gently. I turned and found her standing beside me. She in her cutoffs, which were more worn with each day. She'd discarded her tee shirt, but retained the bikini top, which she filled copiously. She had a blanket draped over her arm, a warm smile upon her face.

'Glad you could make it. They've already picked a spot on the other side of the hill. My aunt's already a little juiced.'

She led the way, I followed. The hill was actually nothing more than a minor incline of about three feet high. On the other side small groups had already set up lawn chairs or had spread out a variety of blankets and quilts.

'Look who I found,' Antoinette announced to the trio of her aunt, Charlie and Enez.

'Well, if it isn't the elusive Matthew,' chimed Enez. She was dressed in a summer dress of pale blue cotton. Her porcelain skin had an alien glow to it. Christine was somewhat overdressed, she treated every outing, no matter how casual, as an opportunity for competition with her fellow females, all of whom were ignorant of the contest.

As Antoinette spread out her blanket Charlie reached into a cooler that rested between him and Christine, he took out a can of beer and tossed it to me. hadn't we been looking at each other, I bet he would've still thrown it otherwise, he'd seemed to have been aiming for my head. Alcohol was forbidden in the park, but the rule had a long triadition of being ignored by both the public and police on the fourth. Perhaps the denial of booze was perceived as unpatriotic. I looked over at Christine sitting in a lawn chair and casting a critical eye upon Antoinette. She took a cigarette from her pack, 'I'm beginning to think I should have made you wear something more modest. Your mother wouldn't approve of you showing so much skin in public.

'As Christine lit her cigarette, Antoinette glanced at me and had rolled her eyes. But her aunt had a point, her niece's ample form was impossible to ignore.

'But my mother isn't here, and besides you're the one who bought me this suit.'

Christine exhaled loudly, 'This is why I'd make a lousy parent, I indulge when I should be disciplining.'

I'd been standing during their brief exchange. Antoinette grabbed my hand and yanked me down beside her. Meanwhile, Christine had produced Antoinette's tee shirt and held it out.

'Please put this on, Anni, I don't want you drawing stares.'

She complied without protest. I'd of course seen her without a stitch so I was free of any pangs of disappointment. As Christine took a drink from a red plastic cup Antoinette had gotten up and knelt down at her aunt's feet.

'Really, aunt Christine, you sometimes act like I've been running wild in the streets when in truth I've been behaving like a perfect angel.

Yes, I said to myself, outwardly you've been but I alone know what a little demon you are. Had that been a grin Charlie had suppressed? Christine smiled maternally, she reached down and tenderly stroked Antoinette's hair, 'You're a dear child, the best niece I could ever wish for.'

She'd said it with complete sincerity. Satisfied with her aunt's gentle praise Antoinette got up and returned to her spot beside me.

It was somewhat odd interacting with Antoinette under those circumstances. I watched the way she behaved with Christine and sensed genuine affection between them. She only spoke to Charlie and Enez when she had to, but always politely and without a hint of sass. Antoinette helped keep the mood festive, even Charlie seemed agreeable. Only Enez remained somewhat distant to all but Christine.

By nine the sky had grown suitably dark and the fireworks began. Antoinette and I had ended up sitting in identical positions, legs stretched straight out, our torsos leaning backward while we used our arms as support.

It was during those multicolored explosions that flowered in the night sky to the exclamations of the crowd that I felt it, Antoinette's pinky as it lightly brushed against mine. That diminutive display of affection lasted mere seconds, so fast as to almost not have happened at all. Still, it had caused a spark of excitement to surge through my body. For just a moment I launched a glance at her from the corner of my eye, saw her face bathed in light: red, yellow, green.

Unknown to us that had been the moment we'd been discovered. My sweet Antoinette, her tiny gesture inadvertently triggered a series of treacheries. I became set on a perilous side path. But at that time Antoinette and I were still ignorant of the viper in our midst.

The evening drew to its conclusion, I exchanged liquor-induced warm and fuzzy farewells. Enez released me with a wave and forced smile, the mirror had acquired another crack. I walked alone under a cloudless sky, still unawares. Midway home I'd once again became touched with the feeling that I was being watched.

Chapter Thirty

That following Sunday afternoon I was paid an unexpected visit by Christine. I'd received her with some apprehension, but after some friendly replaying of the fireworks she cheerfully asked if I could help her solve a minor dilemma that had arisen and the feeling evaporated. I invited her in and over drinks she relayed her problem.

It turned out she and Charlie had accepted an invitation to spend a week at a cabin belonging to one of Charlie's friends. They were supposed to leave within a week.

'We accepted months ago and I'm afraid it's completely slipped my mind.'

Christine took out a cigarette and placed it between her lips. I lit it for her. 'What's to keep you from going?'

She exhaled smoke and grinned broadly. 'You're such a gentleman. Well, you see, it's Antoinette. When I agreed to her staying with me I'd already forgotten my previous commitment.'

'Why not take her along?'

'I considered that, but there will be no children her age staying with us. You know how easily teenagers become bored.'

'You could bring one or both of the Derbyfield girls.'

'I thought of that as well, seems they'll be visiting their grandparents.'

We both became quiet. I watched Christine, something was turning in that brain of hers. I was about to make the most ridiculous suggestion when Christine opened her mouth and said, 'I'd been thinking, perhaps it would be all right to let Anni stay by herself. I'd hate to put you on the spot, but I'd like to hear your opinion.'

I had to stifle the urge to let out a burst of crazed laughter. In a voice of complete calm I offered my answer.

'Antoinette seems, to me at least, to be very mature for her age. I'm sure you can consider her completely trustworthy.'

Relief washed over her face. 'I'm so glad to hear you say that. You know the whole time she's been under my roof she hasn't caused me a lick of trouble.'

Then she followed up with a request, 'I'd just like to ask you the tiniest of favors. Would you check on her from time to time? I agree, she's completely trustworthy, it's some of the neighborhood boys I'm worried about. It would really ease my mind.'

The absurdity of what she'd just asked of me was of course lost on the poor woman. Had she known of Antoinette's and my numerous trysts she would have had me put behind bars. Instead she'd offered the fox the very keys to the henhouse.

Later that night as we lay beside each other I'd relayed the details of Christine's visit.

'My poor, ignorant auntie, delivering me into the hands of my monster. I suppose you'll want to come over and violate me in her bed.'

When I reminded her that Christina and Charlie had no doubt been intimate in said bed Antoinette's revulsion was instantaneous.

'Oh god, why'd you have to say that!? Just the idea of them going at it like a pair of farm animals.'

She raised herself slightly and propped her chin in the palm of her hand.

'I've a better idea, you and I in a sea of teddy bears.'

I was contemplating the image of a nude Antoinette atop a pile of stuffed animals when she let out one of those sighs that signaled her desire for my full attention.

'What's on your mind?'

'Well, it just occurred to me tht we've been handed a rare opportunity. My aunt and chuckles will be gone for an entire week. Couldn't we arrange our own little private getaway?'

Her proposition had definite appeal, but I felt the need to point out an obvious drawback.

'Won't Christine call the house to check up on you?'

'Don't worry, she won't. Remember, you've been appointed temporary guardian.'

'How can you be so sure?'

'Because I'm the best niece she could ever wish for.'

I found this explanation inexplicably acceptable. I then told her I'd begin making arrangements the next day. Her twin sapphires looked at me and she smiled in a way that was deceptively innocent. I knew it would be another night of testing my endurance.

Chapter Thirty One

After breakfast I'd phoned Carpenter, explained my designs and asked if he could offer any assistance.

'I apologize for any inconvenience, but this opportunity just fell out of the blue.'

'No apology is necessary, such is the nature of our existence, we must grab the brass rings as they come.'

It turned out my timing was fortuitous as the organization owned numerous properties designated for such purposes. One, named 'Summer Isle' was available due to a sudden cancellation. The intended renter had been seriously injured in an automotive accident.

Carpenter went on to describe the location, 'It's a one bedroom cottage that looks out onto Lake Opal, very private, you'll not have to worry about unwanted intrusions. We're sure you'll find it very much to your liking.'

He then explained that all I was required to do was provide a list of preferred foods, specialty items and other necessities. We'd find everything already stocked when we arrived. After he'd informed me that detailed directions would be delivered later in the day we concluded our business.

Chapter Thirty Two

The day before Christine and Charlie's departure I gave into yet another foolish notion and took Antoinette on a shopping trip. We entered the doors of the more expensive shops and boutiques where I indulged her every whim. Whatever piece of clothing or shiny bauble that caught her fancy was immediately purchased. It didn't matter that she'd never have the chance to wear everything I'd bought, I'd simply taken joy in spoiling her.

At no time did I make a misstep, I'd found a certain gratification in my restraint and the various clerks treated us with consideration. Antoinette favored things that allowed her to display generous amounts of her tanned flesh. When no one was watching she teased me by striking provocative poses and throwing sultry looks.

I'd realized while watching my beautiful little fiend that I alone recognized Antoinette for what she was. As she stood beside me at the counter while I was paying for our final purchases, she'd looked at me with a bright smile and asked, 'On the way home can we stop for ice cream?' And just for a moment she seemed like just another innocent little girl.

Chapter Thirty Three

We departed for Summer Isle on the morning of Friday, July 13. Christine and Charlie had left town the previous day. Antoinette propped her bare feet on the car's dash board. I continuously stole glances at her tanned legs and her toes, nails freshly painted a light pink, as they curled and uncurled. All the while the radio played yesterday's hit parade.

We stopped only once during our journey, for lunch at a hamburger stand; it'd been the kind of place I'd thought had long anished from the landscape. The food had been quite good and was served by a woman in her late 40s. Her nametag said her name was Yvonne, she wore a pink uniform and her frosted hair was piled high on her head. She called Antoinette and I hon and thankfully didn't enquire about our destination or the nature of our relationship.

Once back on the road we drove with the windows down, the wind whipped Antoinette's hair about helter skelter and it mixed the sound of her laughter. There were times when Antoinette attempted to lure me into intimacies while I drove. I was able to resist her provocations, but not the sweet pain of arousal. she pouted with disappointment, but I pointed out the many dangers involved including erratic driving, which could possibly lead to an encounter with the police or a tree. Of course I kept my tone soft, I knew all of this was play to her, still she did manage to steal several kisses.

Eventually we exited the highway and onto a seldom used backroad. It was then I'd first taken notice of atmospheric shift, the world seemed more serene now that we found ourselves away from our fellow man. Antoinette remarked on how it'd been over an hour sense we'd seen another car.

I'd turned the radio off, neither of us spoke. I'd been told silence was required when trying to spot the emblem of the nymph. It was the sign we'd reached the hidden entrance to a private road that would take us to Summer Isle.

I'd already slowed the car to roughly 15 miles an hour, we'd already traveled a mile or so when Antoinette shouted excitedly, 'There it is.'

She pointed towards an elm tree and I brought the car to a gentle halt. There, carved into the trunk of the tree was the image of a young girl with delicate wings. It'd been so subtly rendered one could have easily passed it.

I exited the car and walked to the left side of the tree where I'd been told I'd find a hidden gate. In fact, it had been quite invisible to the naked eye and it took me a couple of minutes to find the latch that would open it. With Antoinette behind the wheel I guided the car across the inlet and closed the gate.

We drove along a stretch of narrow path, Antoinette hung her upper body out the window, her hair gently wind blown. To both sides were impenetrable forest, above us clear sky. Antoinette let out a whistle before she brought herself back inside and settled beside me. I'm sure we both felt the same pangs of anticipation.

The path continued for several miles, at the end of which was Summer Isle itself. There were no signs or markings to announce our arrival. Instead the vista at once opened wide, to an azure plain of sky, more vibrant than I'd ever seen before or since.

I looked to my right where I got my first view of the cottage that would be our house for the week. Modest in appearance, slightly elevated to enhance the view of the water from the wooden deck that ran along all four sides of the little building constructed of pale brick. Steps led down a path to the white sanded beach and the clear, inviting waters of Lake Opal.

The entire panoramic seemed unreal, it was as if I was looking at an animated painting. It was a wide open space, but somehow retained the intimate quality Carpenter had promised. It also possessed a secretive trait, as if we'd crossed into a pocket dimension where all of humanity had vanished save Antoinette and I.

I'd barely brought the car to a stop when Antoinette opened her door, jumped out and dashed madly towards the water. When she'd reached the water's edge she stripped down to her underwear. She stood, legs spread, arms outstretched, a pose she retained for a few moments before she charged forward into the incoming waves.

I'd removed my shoes and socks then walked to the spot where Antoinette had deposited her clothes. I sat down on the sand and watched as she'd submerge herself and then burst to the surface sending a fountain of water into the air.

It was only after she'd expended her energy that she finally returned to land. Antoinette's wet skin glistened in the sun, her chest heaved as she regained her breath. She fell to her knees before me, her face radiant.

'Isn't it wonderful?' she asked before falling into my arms. I held her close, slowly her breathing calmed. We spent much of the next hour in silence and gazing out at the beauty that surrounded us.

Later, after we'd unpacked, I followed Antoinette as she explored the cottage's interior, her bare feet softly padded along the wood floor. She went from room to room, peaked in closets and drawers opened kitchen cabinets and ran the tips of her fingers against the furniture. The décor wasa tastfully sparse, everything seemed to have a purpose. I noticed the absence of a television, but there was an old fashioned cabinet radio. At times Antoinette had looked over her shoulder at me, her expression that of a curious child, this same girl who'd earlier thrown herself into the water with abandon.

When our tour had finally concluded Antoinette stretched, her mouth opened wide as she emitted a loud yawn.

'I'm so tired all of a sudden,' she'd said rubbing her eyes. She drowsily wrapped her arms around my waist and pressed the side of her face against my chest while I stroked her hair. The long drive couple with Summer Isle overwhelming beauty made Antoinette's exhaustion contagious. I picked her up and carried her to the bedroom. She was almost completely limp when I laid her down. I removed her still damp bra and panties then undressed myself. When I settled in, she drew me to her and we coupled, tenderly and slow. Afterward she curled up close, within minutes we'd fallen into a deep sleep.

Chapter Thirty Four

That first morning I'd awoken early, I sat at the edge of the bed and looked down at the still sleeping Antoinette, transfixed by the sight of her body at rest.

She lay on her face. My eyes moved from her shoulder down her back where I counted the four tiny moles randomly sprinkled upon her skin. As she began to stir she reached around to scratch one of her shoulder blades with the thumb of her right hand; I saw the palm was pink, one of the few areas of her body untouched by the sun. She then performed a kind of ritual that Id' witnessed before. It involved bending both legs in the air followed by the tapping of the bottom of her foot with the top of the other.

Fully awoken she turned on her side and drew the sheet up to her chin. Antoinette rubbed the sandman out of her eyes, a faint smile creased her face when she saw me. She took my hand and gently tugged it in a silent request for me to lay down beside her. She kissed the fingers of that same hand as she caressed my face.

Antoinette then asked me a question I was completely unprepared for.

'Are you happy being with me?'

'Of course, I've never been happier.'

'Even though, if you were with someone else there wouldn't be any risk?'

Our age gap had never before been a topic of serious discussion.

'There's risk in any relationship, what matters is that I …'

Antoinette cut me off by placing her hand over my mouth.

'No, don't say it.'

I was mystified by her reaction, she had her head bent down slightly.

'I know how you feel, and I feel the same way. But it's just a word people say, most of the time they don't really mean it.'

'But you should hear it out loud at least once.'

I lifted her chin up so she'd meet my gaze.

'Please let me say it, just this once.'

I could see her eyes welling up, she gave me a slight nod.

'I love you Antoinette Mouse.'

At the sound of her name Antoinette squeezed her eyes shut. A single, thin tear emerged, it slid down her cheek. When I tried to wipe it away she wouldn't permit me.

Antoinette wasn't insecure and she wasn't the type that needed constant reassurance, so this display of vulnerability was unusual. She pulled me on top of her. I can still remember her warm breath in my ear, how her hair smelled of greenwood, and the desperate way she clung to me.

Chapter Thirty Five

Later that day I sat on the beach watching Antoinette as she swam. She stood up in the water, which came up to her knees. She wore a bikini I'd bought for her, light blue with pink, yellow and white accents. She reached down and adjusted the waist band. It was a simple, unconscious act on her part, but combined with her water slicked hair and sunkissed skin it provided a precious moment for me. It would be a memory I'd cling to in my darkest hours. Even then I wondered, how many more of these gifts would I receive?

The realization that Antoinette would eventually be returned to the arms of her parents was allowed to creep its way into my thoughts. The vision of her shifting her bikini bottom threatened to transform into a thorn puncturing my heart. I knew then that the only way I could retain my sanity was by denying reality. Life without Antoinette was something I dared not imagine.

Antoinette, eleven years my junior. Antoinette slippery when wet. Antoinette my adolescent eroticism. Despite my best efforts I couldn't completely restrain my tears. When Antoinette asked I told her the sun had gotten in my eyes.

Chapter Thirty Six

We'd just finished lunch and had settled in the hammock strung between two trees behind the cottage. We took at least one nap a day, always after lunch, the sound of the gentle back and forth would lull us to sleep. But this time I felt Antoinette's eyes on me, even though my own remained closed.

'Matthew, tell me about your first love,' she said quietly before resting her head on my chest. Of course, I couldn't tell her about Alison, my one true secret. So, I told her about Lisa Wheeler, 16 years old, my babysitter. Lisa, shoulder length black hair, hazel eyes and strawberry lip gloss. How she wore sweaters in the fall and winter, a volleyball uniform in spring and shorts in summer.

I told her about the only day I had Lisa all to myself, how strange it was that I couldn't recall where my family had gone. It was Sunday, late June; the slivers of sunlight coming through the trees as we walked to Manner Park for a picnic.

We ate ham and cheese sandwiches, potato chips and fruit punch while sitting on a red and white checked blanket under an elm tree. She'd had a thin scratch on her left knee that my eyes would return to again and again. Those same legs I sat between as we coasted down a slide and then after slipping off her shoes how they were high in the air as she propelled herself on a swing, bare toes pointing upward. How she smiled when she looked over at me. The sound of squeaking metal, our shadows on the ground.

It was while we were on our way back, I'd been running, perhaps too fast, when I stumbled and fell down on the sidewalk and skinned my knee. Although, it hurt I put on a brave face, I wasn't about to cry in front of Lisa. She helped me to my feet, blood was already trickling down my leg. Of course, it was an injury that looked much worse than it actually was. Once home Lisa took me into the bathroom and had me sit on the edge of the bathtub. She cleaned my wound with a damp cloth and after she'd placed a bandage on my knee she gave it a quick kiss to make it all better.

Two months later Lisa moved with her family to Arizona. Her departure came as a shock, she might as well have died. Perhaps if I'd been given a photo or some other kind of memento her leaving wouldn't have been so traumatic. I suppose most would've labeled my attachment to Lisa a child's crush. The word crush is a verb, it means to force by pressure so as to damage or injure.

Antoinette had silently listened to reminiscences. After I'd finished I'd opened my eyes and she was again looking down at me with benevolent eyes. She bent down and kissed me on the forehead, then said, 'Matthew, you're a lost little boy.'

She hadn't said it in a tone of mockery. She realized I'd just confessed my discovery of life's random cruelty. She placed her head back on my chest and we soon dozed off.

Chapter Thirty Seven

It was during our second night at Summer Isle that I had the dream, at least that's what I'd believed it was at the time. I'd already begun to realize there were aspects of my Antoinette that were best described as cryptic.

In this vision I was awoken, but whoever wakes up in a dream? This was one of the reasons for my doubts. It was by the sound of a girl's laughter that'd roused me. Antoinette was not beside me in bed, nor did I find her anywhere inside the cottage. Eventually, I was lured outside by the laughter that continued during my search.

I stepped out onto the deck to a starless, black velvet sky, but with a full moon that appeared larger than normal. On the beach raged a massive bonfire, its flames reaching right, but into the air and reflecting off of the lake's mirror surface. Even at a distance I could feel its heart on my skin, it grew more intense as I stepped off the deck and walked toward it.

I was mere feet away when Antoinette emerged from the fire. She was nude, her eyes glowing like a nocturnal animal. A humming sound began to ring in my ears. As it transformed into something resembling a drumbeat, Antoinette began to dance. Her movements became more hedonistic as the drumming intensified and the fire raged, despite its heat on my body, I felt no urge to shield myself.

Antoinette ceased her cavorting and had begun to move towards me, her naked body glowing like smelted metal, the expression on her face was a mask of torrid sensuality.

'Matthew, ever since I first spied on you I knew I had to have you for my very own,' she said, along with some other words I didn't understand, but had sounded like backward speech. She took my face in her glowing hands and pressed her lips to mine. As in my previous reverie I felt myself being consumed, yet the sensation caused no fear only a desire for total submission. I awoke suddenly, my body tingling. I opened my eyes and saw Antoinette, she was sitting up looking at me and smiling in the most peculiar manner.

Chapter Thirty Eight

By our third day a routine had been established. Antoinette and I would awake between 10:30 and 11:00 in the morning, she'd immediately satisfy her craving that always left both our brows damp with sweat. After washing we'd take in a light breakfast outdoors on the deck. We prepared all our meals together, seldom using silverware when eating.

Our days were spent enjoying simple activities. We went swimming and on exploratory hikes. Antoinette had discovered a scrabble game in our bedroom closet and we played while sipping fruit drinks spiked with rum. She was quite adept and won most of our matches. There were many spontaneous couplings filled with mutual gratification. My arousal made easy by the fact that on most days She wore nothing but her bathing suit, the same one that had brought that bittersweet pang to my heart. For some reason I felt no urge to disclose my dream and neither of us mentioned those odd first moments after my waking.

It was sometime in the middle of the week after Antoinette had just exited the water. I'd handed her a towel and while she rested on her knees drying her hair I realized we hadn't spotted a single boat or plane in our entire stay. When I casually remarked on this she responded with a shrug of her shoulders.

There was one more episode that gave rise in me a feeling of misgiving. It happened on our next to last day at Summer Isle. We'd been on one of our walks when we came upon a previously undiscovered trail, so narrow we barely had enough room to walk side by side. Also odd was that the surrounding woods had become completely devoid of the usual bird sounds, the only noise coming from our footsteps.

The path came to an abrupt end where, of all things, a rock wall had been constructed. It stood approximately five feet high and 15 feet in length. Inexplicable in its purpose and no clues as to why anyone would have felt the need to erect it. And yet Antoinette seemed drawn to it. I watched as she silently approached and placed her hands upon it. As she gently caressed the stones with her fingers she knelt down on one knee and placed her ear to it. The impression was that she was listening to a voice only she could hear. She remained like this for perhaps a minue before she broke away and returned to my side.

Neither of us spoke as we made our way back towards the beach. Antoinette held onto my hand, a bit firmer than usual. She didn't appear upset, instead her mood seemed contemplative, as if she was trying to understand an important, if not fully comprehended, revelation.

It was after we'd left the woods and stood on the shore that whatever had perplexed her left. Before we'd started our way back to the cottage I thought I spied something in the distance, a figure, or so it seemed. It very well could have been some vegetation, or even a mirage. But I felt convinced it was human. My attention was drawn away by Antoinette as she pulled my arm. Soon I was more involved with the sight of the water as it lapped against her feet.

Chapter Thirty Nine

On our last morning at Summer Isle we awoke early and silently ate breakfast on the deck. It was as if speaking aloud would shatter the peace, even when we touched it seemed like a gentle accident.

The sun hadn't completely ascended so the color palette of our surroundings was beautifully askew. The cloudless sky was a pale pink while the water below was a darker, more foreboding blue. The beach resembled the lunar surface, the remains of a sand castle we'd built earlier in the week seemed strangely out of place on an otherwise flat surface. We were surrounded by a scene of vivid charm, just as it had been on our arrival, but it seemed to be already mourning our departure.

Antoinette had chosen to wear white, a long sleeved top with a v-neck and a matching short skirt. I knew she'd miss Summer Isle even more than I. She seemed to belong there. When she quietly rose from her chair and descended the steps for one last walk on the beach I didn't follow. She didn't seem to desire company. She took her time absorbing the details of the landscape, the faint breezes caused her bangs and the hem of her skirt to flutter against her skin.

Even at a distance I could see the melancholy in her face. Antoinette sat down on a log, she rested her chin on her knees and studied her sand covered feet. As she brushed the grit away I viewed it as an act of despondency. Antoinette and her week of wonders was drawing to a close.

When she stood and began to walk back towards the cottage I got up and met her at the top of the steps. I wrapped my arms around her, she was shivering slightly.

'Do you know what this reminds me of?' she asked.

'No.'

'The weekend I spent at my Grandmother's four years ago. It was a humid afternoon so I was wearing a summer dress. I'd just stepped out the back door and was walking down the stone path that led to a stream that ran behind the house. Halfway along the path I stopped and looked back. I don't know why. That's when I saw the red spots, they went from the door to where I was standing. Then I noticed the blood running down my leg. Later that day my Grandmother told me I was no longer a child, that from now on I'd see the world through a different set of eyes.'

Antoinette looked down at the beach, 'I'll never forget this place,' she said with finality. She then went inside, her head slightly lowered.

After the car had been packed we took a minute for a last look before our departure. During our entire stay we'd not taken a single photograph. It didn't seem like Summer Isle's beauty could have been captured on film. All Antoinette and I would have were our memories, and they seemed designed to fade.

Chapter Forty

Days later I was at the supermarket, I wandered the aisles, somewhat preoccupied by thoughts of the odd episodes that had occurred on Summer Isle. I'd become lost in a juxtaposition of images. My dream of Antoinette at the fire, the stone wall and the mysterious figure I'd convinced myself was real. Although our holiday had been filled with happiness I still found it difficult to jettison my thoughts of those miner aberrations.

'Well, imagine meeting you here of all places.' The words sounded like they were coming from the bottom of a well. I didn't respond, but instead continued to stare at the jars of pasta sauce. They reminded me of Antoinette's menstrual blood.

'Matthew, did you hear me?'

I snapped out of my daydream. In front of me stood Christine, her hair done, in full makeup and wearing a dress and heels. She was a ridiculous contrast to the other women who appeared pallid under the fluorescent lights.

'I'm sorry, I was lost in my thoughts,' the words fell out of my mouth.

'Oh, I understand, you artists are always off in your little worlds. Must make this mundane existence of ours more tolerable.'

'Yes, I suppose so,' I offered feebly, although Christine didn't seem to take notice. It was odd to see her without the usual combination of drink and cigarette. I'd begun to feel increasingly foolish and tried to deflect the conversation.

'How was your trip, I hope you and Charlie enjoyed yourselves,' I asked as she placed a jar of olives in her cart. I saw the only other items were tampons and a fifth of vodka.

'It was a giggle, but of course I've already told you all about it. But I did want to thank you again for calling and telling me how Antoinette was behaving herself.'

What was she talking about? Perhaps she'd suffered some alcohol-induced hallucination.

'Now, I don't want to seem rude, but I really have to shake a tail feather. Charlie's waiting for me.'

'Of course.'

'You really must come to dinner again, Enez has been pestering me for weeks to have another get together. I'll call you soon.'

Christine turned and shimmied off, the heels of her shoes echoing dully. I watched her disappear around a corner before I went in the opposite direction.

The next thing I can remember was standing beside my car trying to catch my breath. The air outside felt thick and pungent. I tasted bile in my throat and I became worried that I might vomit in public. Five minutes passed before I felt calm enough to drive home. I'd begun to feel like an actor in a play, but the only member of the cast without a complete script.

Chapter Forty One

Two days after my encounter with her aunt Antoinette unexpectedly fell ill. It would turn out to be a minor bout of food poisoning and she would recover within 24 hours. But it left an opening in which a harlot of destruction was allowed to reenter my life.

That day had begun normally. I'd awoken to the sun and a cloudless blue sky. Birds sang, a dog barked and children played while their mothers tended their gardens.

My phone rang, normally I ignored it, but for some unknown reason I'd answered. Had I known what this routine act was about to trigger I'd have ripped the cord from the wall.

It was Passolini. He'd become aware that I'd begun growing bored with writing screenplays, more specifically scripts for him. This did not surprise him, he'd long ago established a formula with his films, one his fans expected him to stick to. Lately he'd been suggesting I should switch my energy to producing.

'That's where the true excitement lies, not to mention the money,' he'd stated. Passolini knew I didn't need the money. But the challenges involved I found appealing. Looking back I wondered if I had been anticipating Antoinette's enviable departure, knowing I'd need something to keep me busy. He invited me to dinner with a possible investor. Normally, I'd have declined, but Antoinette's temporary malady left me with a hole to fill, so I consented to join him.

Passolini collected me shortly before night. As I climbed into the backseat of his limousine I was greeted with the sight of our potential money man.

Elton Highroad was snorting a line of cocaine off his left hand, in his right hand he held a glass of scotch while a half-smoked joint smoldered in an ashtray. He wore a Gucci suit jacket over a white shirt with the top three buttons undone, designer jeans and his sockless feet were encased in an expensive looking pair of loafers. Despite the fact the sun had begun to set, and the limo's windows being tinted, Elton wore sunglasses. They would remain on his face the entire night.

After introductions were made in which I got a good look at his capped teeth, Elton generously offered to share his drugs with us. Passolini and I both declined but did accept a whiskey on the rocks. From his accent I guess Elton was of middle-eastern ancestry, but his name didn't fit, I wondered if it was a kind of alias.

After a twenty minute drive, where among other things I learned Sophia had gone into rehab, we exited the freeway and entered the city limits. It'd been a place I'd taken great steps to avoid ever since I'd returned home. It always reminded me of an aging beauty queen in that, if one could be bothered, you could almost see the former majesty. But I rarely bothered, if at all.

Many of the skyscrapers stood dark and unoccupied. Its streets were practically deserted with only the occasional pair of black teenagers or homeless man. Liquor stores were on nearly every street corner and I saw a parade of wig shops, fast food restaurants and storefront churches.

We finally arrived at our destination, the Lelander hotel, an eight story souvenir from the 1940s. Like the vacant train station to the south it should've been demolished decades ago. But like so much of the city it'd stubbornly refused to perish with any sense of grace.

We entered through revolving doors, as we climbed up marble stairs that led to the lobby I was greeted with an unexpected sight. It wasn't the ramshackled interior I'd expected. I'd later learn that a major innovation had been financed by a well-monied widow. She'd no doubt spent her flapper days performing the Charleston on its dining room tables.

Passolini had made reservations at the hotel's restaurant, a type of steakhouse that'd recently come into vogue. A décor of dark wood paneling and circular booths upholstered in red leather under dim lighting; it was meant to give the place a clubhouse ambiance, instead it felt like we'd just entered a funeral home.

All three of us ordered the filet minion, Elton never touched his. Between his frequent trips to the men's room he downed one scotch after another while talking a blue streak. The topics ranged from his recent vacation to St. Bart's, the home in Greece he'd just bought (he'd overpaid) and the British heiress he was dating. The topic of motion pictures was never mentioned. It was during one of Elton's absences that Passolini informed me that movies would not be discussed, this was, in his words, the getting acquainted phase.

Two hours later when the check arrived Passolini paid it. One of the first things I'd learned about the idle rich is that they never pay for anything, because they never carry cash or credit cards.

Once we were back in that enormous lobby I was informed of the real reason Elton had selected the Lelander. There was a fetish ball being held on the second floor and Elton, being the decadent he was, wanted to attend.

'I've always been fascinated by the various ways unattractive people have devised to copulate,' he said with a reptilian grin before setting off for the elevator.'

I'd reluctantly followed, Passolini seemed to consider it part of the price of doing business. As the elevator ascended I summoned images of Antoinette lying in my bed, her tanned skin wrapped in clean, white sheets.

When we stepped out onto the second floor I was greeted by the aroma of body odor mixed with lubricant and forced excess. It seemed to perk up Elton even more.

At the entrance to the ballroom I noticed a sign had been posted informing us that fetish attire was required in order to gain entry. My momentary relief was dashed by Passolini and a few well-place hundred dollar bills.

Once inside I found the place despondent, my ears were assaulted by the cacophony that streamed from massive speakers mounted on the walls. We made our way through a crowded dance floor jammed with bodies dressed in latex and black leather. A strobe light was activated, which elevated the scene to nightmare status.

Elton had quickly located the bar which was tended by a woman, her hair shaved into a mowhawk that'd been dyed blood red and gelled into nasty looking spikes. She was topless, but her nipples were covered with strips of black tape.

Before she could take my order I'd excused myself and went in search of the men's room. Thankfully, it was easy to find. The only other people inside were a pair of men dressed identically in leather pants and biker boots. Both were shirtless and had their heads shaved. They stood in a corner only giving me a momentary glance before returning to their hushed conversation. While I was relieving myself I thought I heard noises coming from the stall doors. I concluded my business as quickly as possible and left.

I'd returned to find a drink waiting for me. I picked it up and took a swallow without thinking. When it hit my taste buds I recognized it as absinth. I immediately sat the glass down, but the damage had been done. I knew then that the evening wouldn't end without my suffering some consequence.

My vision had begun to blur around the edges. I looked over at Passolini who was deep into conversation with Elton, but I couldn't hear what they were saying. The din had become an auditory wall. I realized I'd lost control of my environment. I attempted to once again summon images of Antoinette, but only succeeded in drawing brief flashes that I couldn't hold onto. The people who surrounded me became increasingly grotesque. Some had collars around their necks to which chains were attached so they could be led about like dogs. Others had masks of tattoos and piercings. Their eyes seemed cynical and devoid of empathy. I felt a jaded under current running through the hedonism.

Time skipped. I'd wandered off and away from Passolini and Elton, and found myself watching a plump man who'd been strapped into an upright, spread eagle position. His buttocks were covered with welts, the result of the beating he was receiving at the hands of a woman wielding a cricket bat.

At first her face remained hidden in shadows, but I could still discern her outfit. Black, arm-length gloves, corset, panties and thigh-high boots. A sexualized Gestapo officer who used her instrument with zeal. She'd ceased her work on the fat man and had stepped into a stray shaft of light, her hair was the first thing I saw. Cut into a short bob, that awful hue, like a brand new penny. Our eyes met and I found myself staring into a cracked mirror.

'Why Matthew, you seem out of sorts,' said Enez Sparrow.

She then stepped forward and touched my cheek with one of her gloved hands. I remember I flinched.

Chapter Forty Two

Enez and I stared at each other for an indeterminate amount of time, it was she who finally broke the silence.

'I could use a drink, you on the other hand seem to have had enough. Now, come along, I've been meaning to speak with you.'

I silently followed Enez back to the bar, people seemed to instinctively move out of her way. She ordered a glass of red wine. I waved the bartender away, the mouthful of absinth along with the drinks I'd consumed at dinner had put me at a disadvantage, my head had begun to throb and I felt sweat forming along my spine. I searched for Passolini and Elton, but they'd disappeared. Enez produced a small, silver case she'd hidden in one of her boots, From it, she extracted a black cigarette. She lit it and as she drew in her first inhalation I made my eyes focus on the orange glow burning on the cigarette tip in an attempt to collect my wits. When Enez blew smoke, I smelled cloves.

'I didn't know you smoked.'

It'd made no sense to utter that aloud, but I was attempting, however weakly, to urge Enez to get on with it. Each moment I stayed in that place felt like another nail in my coffin.

'I only indulge the habit on special occasions.'

I refused to take the bait and let the remark hang in the air. Enez was obviously trying to prolong my discomfort so I'd instantly grasped a strategy of remaining as tight lipped as possible. I sat in silence watching her smoke and take tiny sips from her glass. My message was clear, she'd have to earn her tribute. After a long minute had passed and half her cigarette burned Enez finally picked up her narration.

'I can still remember the night we met at Christine's, when she remarked on her belief that little Antoinette was, to use her words, having a little romance. The notion sparked my curiosity. I must confess. I enjoy sticking my nose in other people's business. A bad habit, I know, just can't help myself. Antoinette is at that age and yet I just couldn't imagine her wasting time on one of the local boys with their bad skin and protruding adam's apples. She is, after all, exceptional.'

I feel myself longing for a glass of ice water, but I didn't want to take my eyes off of Enez for even a second. Who knew what else she'd had hidden in her boots.

'The comings and goings of Christine's niece really that interesting? Didn't think you had the time to waste.'

Enez tapped her cigarette sending a chunk of ash towards my feet.

'It wasn't, and I didn't. I was surprised by your rejection, call me thin skinned, but I'm not used to hearing 'no.' I felt hurt and didn't like it.'

For a brief moment I saw a flash of sadness before the anger returned. Antoinette had been correct in her assessment of Enez's character. She finished her glass and signaled the bartender for a second. After it had been delivered Enez continued.

'Several weeks later when I attended Passolini's wrap party and met Sophia whom I'm sure you remember. Seemed like I wasn't the only one to feel your sting. It was odd because I was certain you were not gay and sex with Sophia came with no strings attached. A piece of the puzzle was missing. I was perplexed for weeks.'

Enez took a drink. When she set her glass down it was half full. I hoped my mock indifference was having an effect.

'But it was sweet Antoinette who'd finally provide the answer to the riddle and it was a real eureka moment. It was on the Fourth of July.'

It'd been the feline in her, remove the paw long enough for her prey to catch its breath before pinning it down again.

'At first I'd thought you were just being nice, indulging her with some mild flirting. You were very careful, not letting your eyes linger on her, admittedly impressive, figure. It must have been torture, having her so close. Later, when the fireworks were popping and I saw that pinky of hers brush up against yours. It happened so quick, it was luck that allowed me to witness it. Christine didn't catch it, I doubt she would've realized the significance. I suppose I shouldn't have been surprised, Antoinette does have a certain aura about her. But really, Matthew, she's still a fifteen-year-old girl.'

My mind raced. I asked the simplest, most obvious question I could think of.

'What do you want, Enez?'

She snuffed out her cigarette, which had been smoked to nothing.

'I haven't decided yet, but you can expect to hear from me soon.'

She reached over and pinched my chin with her thumb and forefinger.

'And this time, Matthew, I suggest you pick up the phone.'

She released me with a snap and silently went off to rejoin the fray. I looked at her half empy glass, the smeared lipstick traces on its rim.

I no longer knew nor cared where Passolini or Elton were. I'd somehow made my way out of the mass of humanity and found myself on the sidewalk. I was able to hail a cab. I instructed the driver to take me to a bank machine and then home. He dropped me off at my front door where I entered the house. As I climbed the stairs I'd noticed my breathing had become labored. When I reached my bedroom door I was already sweating heavily. I needed Antoinette, needed her desperately.

Chapter Forty Three

I remained frozen at the door that was opened no more than half an inch, no light or sound came from the other side. I'd closed my eyes before giving it a gentle push. I waited until I was finally able to discern the sound of Antoinette's breathing. I began to inhale and exhale in unison with her, overcome with relief at her quick recovery. Yet, I didn't enter the bedroom. I'd brought my hands up and saw they were shaking. My shirt was glued to my skin, it smelled of sweat and cigarette smoke, and I was certain my breath was equally noxious. I became overcome with the need to wash away the events of the evening. Only then could I permit myself to touch Antoinette.

I removed my shoes and quietly made my way back downstairs, the house contained a full bathroom on each floor. I shut the door and stripped down. I turned on the shower, and I waited for the water to grow hot.

'You seem like the type she'd enjoy pestering,' Charlie's words rang out as I stepped under the water, the temperature caused me to inhale sharply. I was then struck by the realization that discovery had perhaps been inevitable. Charlie's surprise visit had no doubt been prompted by Enez, she'd been the mysterious figure behind the wheel at the foot of my driveway.

I'd been tempting consequence for some time and I'd found myself in the spider's web.

Enez had a pronounced disdain for males, she'd managed to make the outwardly macho Charlie her serf and had no doubt been busy conjuring a series of degradations to inflict upon me. It'd occurred to me as I stood there enveloped in steam that Enez's attitude towards other women wasn't any better. She betrayed Christine and Antoinette's welfare was obviously no concern to her. The more I thought of Enez's nature the more it became apparent she was odious for its own sake.

A revelation came to me, sharp and cold. I had to destroy Enez Sparrow, scrape her off the world's shoe. I stood under the water and envisioned blood pouring form her orifices. I then counted backward from twenty and replaced my murderous thoughts with images of the girl who was sleeping above. I wanted to go beyond, silently I pleaded with her to help me get there.

When I'd finally stepped out of the shower I felt somewhat calmed. I found a towel and dried myself. I left my soiled clothing on the floor and made my way back to my bedroom.

I entered and went to the side of the bed where Antoinette was sleeping. I knelt beside her and waited for my eyes to adjust to the darkness. Soon I was able to make her out. I don't know how long I watched her sleep but eventually she awoke.

'I was feeling better. You weren't here so I decided to wait. Guess I fell asleep,' she said brushing her cheek against the pillow.

I slid into bed beside her. I drew comfort from the smoothness and warmth of Antoinette's skin that was free of ink and piercings, even her ear lobes were untouched. As she rubbed her foot against my leg I felt her slightly calloused sole, the result of so much time spent in bare feet. It was her call to the beast. When my hand went between her legs she let out a sigh of approval then gave me a sign to proceed further, to go beyond.

Chapter Forty Four

When I awoke the next morning Antoinette had gone back to her still ususpecting aunt's. She always left as silently as she arrived, but still retained a presence.

I'd acquired a clarity of purpose and found myself on a road that didn't fork, but instead went in a straight line. I proceeded as such.

I got out of bed, washed, dressed and then went downstairs and fixed breakfast. The previous night had left me with a pronounced appetite.

After I'd eaten my fill I called Passolini. He apologized for last night and expressed his relief that I'd found my way home safely. After I'd assured him I held no animosity I asked a favor. I wanted him to contact his agent, the man who'd spied on me, and have the man get me Enez's home address. Passolini agreed without question.

The man called twenty minutes later with the information. Like his employer he didn't ask why I wanted it. I wrote as he dictated.

It took 20 minutes by car to reach Enezs residence. I saw her silver Mercedes parked in the driveway. I parked across the street four lengths back and waited. I checked my watch, it read a quarter to eleven.

Half an hour later Enez finally emerged. She wore a light coat of pale grey, matching high heels and carried a ridiculously large tote bag made of red vinyl. She tossed it into the back seat of her car and drove off. I started my own can and followed at a safe distance.

Over the course of that afternoon Enez visited four of what I guessed were clients, three men and one woman. They greeted her at the front door and all lived in upper middle class neighborhoods. The men were all middle age, while the woman appeared to be in her mid-twenties. Each appointment lasted for exactly 90 minutes.

I'd stayed in my car and tried to imagine what was happening behind closed doors. Enez being a dominatrix made perfect sense. I wondered if she used her real name or a made-up title, and what could possibly be in that monstrous, red bag?

It was nearly 8:00 in the evening when she finished for the day. I'd chosen not to follow her back home. When I'd heard my stomach growling I realized I hadn't eaten since that morning. I drove to the nearest diner where I wolfed down a club sandwich.

As I drove home I thought of how many people held dual lives, the selves they hid were their true identities. Did Enez and the people she dominate consider me the depraved one? But I'd never been able to convince myself of Antoinette being a normal female and there was a growing body of evidence that proved me correct. I think Enez recognized she was more than a mere child.

Already my plan had begun to gel. I didn't doubt my resolve nor my ability to carry it out. I just hoped I'd be successful in covering my tracks. More importantly, I couldn't leave anything that would in any way even hint at my involvement with Antoinette.

Chapter Forty Five

When I returned home I found Antoinette waiting for me on the patio when she'd been lazily sunning herself.

'Where've you been all day, it's not another woman is it?' she asked before letting out a gale of laughter. I gave her a kiss and went into the kitchen and opened a bottle of champagne. After pouring us each a glass I momentarily went back inside to turn on the stereo. I turned up the volume so the music could drift outdoors. I waited until the Shirelles had finished singing, 'Little Girl' before I raised the Enez problem with Antoinette.

I'd originally planned to keep her ignorant of the situation, but then thought better of it. It'd occurred to me that I'd be guilty of treating her like a child.

The champagne had given me a slight buzz. I gazed into Antoinette's eyes, they made me remember the word fairuza, which was Persian for blue. My hand reached out and began to stroke her leg.

'Antoinette, do you trust me, that I always have our best interests at heart?'

'Of course I do,' she said without hesitation.

I suddenly found it difficult to form the words. She must have sensed this for her brow furrowed slightly. She then took the hand that'd been massaging her leg into hers.

'Matthew, what's the matter?'

When I didn't answer her expression darkened.

'Someone knows about us.' It was a statement not a question.

'Enez,' I said the name like it was a curse.

What Antoinette said next took me aback.

'Goddamn witch, I knew it was her.'

I was confused. Had she harbored suspicions and kept them from me? I asked. The response was not one I'd expected.

'I've always been suspicious of that haughty bitch. The other day, when I was sick, it was from a cherry tart my aunt had given me. It wasn't until later she told me that Enez had brought it over.'

'Why would she want to poison you?'

She gave my hand a little squeeze. 'When I called her a witch I wasn't making a joke. As far as her motivation, there could be more than one. That's the way it is with women like her.'

Our eyes met, I reached up and touched Antoinette's cheek. She responded by kissing my palm.

'I have a plan,' I said.

She said nothing but nodded her head before wrapping her arms around me. I believed then as I believe now that she knew what I was going to do, and that she approved.

Chapter Forty Six

That night I awoke with a start from a nightmare, one so vivid that it caused my body to spring upright.

Antoinette and I were back on Summer Isle's beach and I found myself at the bottom of a pit that had been dug in the sand. She was above me, leaning over the edge with her hand stretched out towards me. But no matter how hard I tried I couldn't reach her. Our fingertips would be within an inch of making contact, but in the end all I succeeded in was to cause more sand to fall into the pit.

Antoinette's expression of desperation changed to one of acceptance. As she rose to her feet I was able to sense what she was about to do. When I tried to discourage her I found I had no voice. She closed her eyes and leapt into the pit, as I caught her in my arms the walls began to collapse around us. It was just before we were completely engulfed that I woke up.

I looked over, Antoinette was still sleeping peacefully beside me. The sight of her calmed me and I silently hoped my bad dream was not an omen of things to come.

Chapter Forty Seven

Over the course of that week I continued my surveillance of Enez's comings and goings, I wanted to familiarize myself with her habits no matter how mundane. IT also provided me with opportunities to ponder my situation.

There'd been a number of strange occurrences since I'd begun my relationship with Antoinette. While I hadn't completely ignored them I'd still set them aside. It was as if examining them too closely would reveal a truth that would prove overwhelming.

The fact I'd opened the door to a new world, one that existed alongside my old one. My new environment had its own set of rules. Antoinette intuitively knew them, perhaps Enez did as well. But I'd have to learn them as I went along, there was simply no other way.

In the eyes of human law and society I was already a guilty man. First of statutory rape of a minor, taking said minor to Summer Isle no doubt would be viewed as kidnapping. Then there was the Bronze Peacock, could it not be considered a criminal enterprise? Murder would be the cherry on top of this concoction. My motivation was fear and self-preservation, it made my decision final. I would kill

Enez Sparrow.

The instrument I'd use was already under the same roof as I. I'd unzipped the leather pouch and taken out the Walther semi-automatic pistol. It felt cold and heavier than I'd remembered. The gun had belonged to my father, his motivation for buying such a weapon had been unknown to me.

On his weekly trips to the firing range I was sometimes allowed to accompany him where he indulged my boyish desire by permitting me to fire the gun at paper targets.

I could still remember the first time I pulled the trigger, the deafening explosion of sound and the force of the recoil. I felt like Zeus tossing bolts of lightning. I'd developed into a reasonably good shot then, but that'd been a decade ago. Until recently I'd completely forgotten the gun's existence.

I brought it downstairs and set it down on the kitchen countertop. Metal against marble, it was the soundof finality. Then just as my father had shown me I went about disassembling the gun and cleaning it.

Chapter Forty Eight

After I'd cleaned and reassembled the Walther I contemplated the need for target practice, but where could I conduct it? The range my father had taken me to was no longer in business, even had it still existed it would've been a foolish risk to practice in public.

'Eveswood,' said Antoinette.

My mischievous little sprite had again materialized silently. I sometimes wondered if she spied on me without my knowledge.

'Eveswood,' I repeated out loud, the name seemed familiar.

'It's a large, wooded area on the eastern edge of town, rather dense, but I know of a hidden path that leads to a clearing.'

Antoinette's previous musings over her ability to read my thoughts had been a confession and not the jest I'd originally taken them for. As with many things that concerned her I found myself accepting it.

'Well, then would you be so kind and write down the directions?'

'No, you'd never be able to find it on your own. You'll have to take me along.'

My first instinct was to argue against the idea. A firearm, not licensed to me, add a fifteen-year-old girl, not an agreeable recipe.

'Matthew, you really can be very silly at times,' she said before delivering me a kiss on tiptoes.

'I wouldn't allow anything bad to happen.'

Once again my concerns were brushed aside.

Our drive to Eveswood went without incident. We found a spot to park that allowed my car to be suitably camouflaged.

Antoinette led the way across a field of tall grass. I carried a blanket over my shoulder and a bag filled with empty tin cans. She held a picnic basket that swayed back and forth, sometimes it gently bumped against her tanned leg. At first the woods in front of us seemed impenetrable, but as we got closer I began to see the merest sliver of an opening.

'Antoinette, how'd you find out about this place?'

She looked back at me, 'I saw it in a dream.' She then took me by the hand.

As we stepped into the woods I recalled the trail we'd found at Summer Isle. It'd clearly been made by the treading of people, but the path at Eveswood seemed to have been formed without such assistance. We were surrounded by a tranquil stillness, I also felt slightly giddy, as if I'd been let in on a secret. Did others know of this place, or was the knowledge Antoinette's and mine alone?

How long our hike had lasted I had no idea. Time seemed unimportant. Eventually, I could see an opening forming, it seemed to be bordered by a halo of light. My hand was still intertwined with Antoinette's. I got the impression we were passing through a series of concentric circles, was she their custodian? I seemed to be in a continual process of revelation.

We crossed the threshold and into another circle, the space appeared to be both one spawned of nature and man-made. To our left was a small pond, a circle within a circle. Directly in front of us was a tree, a species I didn't recognize, but its purple leaves that gave it an air of royalty. Finally to our right was a stone wall.

'Look familiar?' she asked?

Identical I thought. Antoinette released my hand, she set down the picnic basket and then took possession of the bag containing the tin cans. I watched as she removed each one and lined them up side by side atop the wall. I set the blanket down and opened the basket where I'd hidden the Walther.

Antoinette returned from the wall and stepped behind me. As I held the gun I noticed it felt lighter than before. She placed her hands on my shoulders, I lifted my arm and took aim at the first can.

'Matthew, I want you to take a moment and close your eyes.'

I obeyed and she spoke intently.

'I want you to hear nothing but the sound of my voice, the voice of the one who knows you honestly and intimately. Envision in your mind the face of your enemy. Her name is a profanity, her existence an obscenity. See her clearly so you may strike her down.'

I chambered a round.

'Open your eyes, Matthew.'

I did, in front of me and floating inches above the wall were six heads, six Enez heads. They stared back at me, six Enez doll heads. Those eyes which I'd once complimented her now seemed disproportionately large, alien.

In quick succession I took aim and fired. Each bullet left a perfect, black hole the size of a dime in the center of the forehead. They hung in the air for a few seconds before they proceeded to vanish in unison.

Antoinette was no longer standing behind me. I looked over towards the pond, she stood at its edge disrobing. She gazed back at me invitingly before she entered the water.

I placed the gun back inside the basket then went to join her stripping off my own clothing on the way. I submerged myself, the water was warm, fragrant and seemed slightly viscous. Antoinette glided over and wrapped her limbs around me.

I can recall a panorama of images. Antoinette's hair glowing hazily, resembling a gold crown. The pink flower I tucked behind her right ear. Her wet shoulders; the water seemed like perfumed oil. How her breathing became more fervent with the contraction of certain muscles. The moment of our mutual release was painfully sweet. Afterward as we lay together on our blanket, my head resting on her stomach. I realized I'd been copulating with a deity.

That afternoon was like a confection for my soul. It eased a suspicion that had been lurking in my mind, that I'd been slowly losing my grip on my sanity. Actually, I'd been reconfiguring myself to my new reality.

Chapter Forty Nine

It was two nights later I awoke and found myself alone in bed. I looked over at the clock on the nightstand, it read midnight.

At first I thought Antoinette had gone downstairs to fix herself something to eat, them my attention was drawn by the sounds coming from the bedroom window, which I'd left open. I got out of bed and looked out. From where I stood I had an unobstructed view of the patio and backyard.

Antoinette was sitting at the patio table, she was still nude. In her hands was a photograph, even at a distance I was still able to recognize Enez's image. Also laid out on the table top were a small hand mirror, a strip of white ribbon and a glass jar. Antoinette was talking to Enez's photo, but her tone was so low I couldn't make out what she was saying. After her discourse was finished she pressed the photo to the mirror's reflective side, she then used the strip of ribbon to bind them together and placed the bundle in the jar. Antoinette then picked up the jar, she stepped off the patio and walked to the edge of the yard. There she used a small spade to dig a hole. She placed the jar inside and buried it. Her task completed she started back towards the house.

I returned to bed an attempted to feign sleep. I could hear Antoinette as she ascended the stairs. She stopped for a moment before she entered the room. My back was to her as she climbed into bed. She didn't lay down, instead she remained seated. I knew she was watching me.

'Matthew, I know you're awake.'

I couldn't help, but feel embarrassed as I turned over. Her face was somewhat obscured by the darkness. For a time neither of us spoke, we just stared at each other and I'd begun to feel unsettled.

'Antoinette, what are you?'

I don't know why I asked that question, but I realized instantly there was fear in my voice. Antoinette smiled, she then began to speak, her voice just slightly louder than a whisper.

'I'm Antoinette Mouse, I'm 15-years old, born on Christmas day. I'm your teenage lover, your bubble gum slut. I'm the girl of your dreams. I'm the one person you don't have to be afraid of.'

Antoinette reached down and pulled the sheet off of my body. She climbed on top of me, taking my hands and guiding them along her form. I surrendered myself to her and my desires under a chorus of whispered assurances. Afterward I felt it was as if she'd shared some of her power with me.

Chapter Fifty

The following afternoon I finally received a phone call from Enez. During our conversation she attempted to gage my mood but I kept my emotions below the surface. The more she tried to stir them the more I remained aloof. I don't think Enez ever understood that by conducting a relationship with Antoinette I'd already discarded conventional morality. If one finds themselves in a den of thieves then what use is morality? I'd come to realize I couldn't be moral and remain honest. There could only be a dominant so long as there was a willing submissive. I already had a master, and she wasn't going to be so easily replaced

When I'd requested we meet at night she readily agreed, but I'd detected a brittle coolness in her voice. She'd failed on some level, but couldn't understand how.

Our meeting was to take place at nine o'clock. I'd expected her to suggest a public place, but to my slight astonishment she'd asked me to come to her home. As she fed me directions I couldn't help but smile.

I'd begun preparing early by changing into a grey t-shirt, blue jeans and a dark blue windbreaker, the most inconspicuous clothing I could think of. I then gathered a second set of clothes, a pair of leather gloves and a baseball cap. I placed them into a brown paper grocery bag. The Walther I stuck under my belt.

I left my house at a quarter after eight already knowing the exact length of time it would take to reach Enez's neighborhood. There was an unattended parking lot six blocks from her house, I fed three hours-worth of quarters into the meter, retrieved the bag from the back seat and began walking.

Enez resided in a part of town known for its ethnic diversity, non-whites being the dominant. All shared two commonalities, they tended to mind their own business and were wary of caucasions. They tended to not look you in the eye, sometimes going out of their way to act as if they didn't see you at all. That was to my advantage.

But I crossed paths with no one, the cars that drove past were filled with black youths who had their own concerns.

I stepped onto Enez's front porch and rang the doorbell. She answered, a bit too quickly, as if she'd been waiting on the other side.

'You're early.'

'I haven't inconvenienced you, have I?'

'Not at all.' She opened the door wider to admit me inside.

Enez wore a lavender bathrobe, opened just enough to show a hint of her breasts. She wasn't unattractive, perhaps when I was younger and lacked experience Enez would've held some allure. But Antoinette had long ago vanquished my desire for other females so completely that they seemed synthetic by comparison.

After Enez shut the door she motioned for me to follow her. She didn't ask me about the bag I held in my hand. As I walked behind her I took notice of her home's interior, which had been decorated with several objects of occult significance. I recalled she'd mentioned her embrace of certain pagan practices.

We entered Enez's bedroom, before she sat down at her dressing table she turned on a radio, out of which came the noise that passes for modern music. Although I found it irritating it served a purpose for the events that unfolded.

Enez sat down in front of a large oval mirror and began applying eye make-up. I sat on the edge of her bed. I made sure I wasn't reflected in the mirror's surface. She still hadn't commented on the bag, which I'd placed at my feet. It had been as if she hadn't seen it.

'So, Matthew, I've always wanted to know, are the Bronze Peacock gatherings as opulent as I've been led to believe?'

It was a question clearly meant to throw me off balance, and it nearly succeeded because her knowledge of the organization came as a surprise. Inwardly, I panicked, but only momentarily.

'I've only attended one function, but yes, it was quite impressive.'

'Did Antoinette enjoy herself?'

'More than I.'

Enez inspected her eyes while a malignant smile crossed her face.

'That group isn't the well-kept secret its members believe it to be. I've many clients whose tastes span a wide spectrum. Men, you're so cute with your little sins. I've come to the conclusion that you engage in your shenanigans just so you can confess to them later.'

I felt the time had come for me to pluck a few strings.

'As long as we're exchanging intimacies may I ask you a question?'

'Of course.'

'Are you having an affair with Charlie?'

Enez let out a short burst of laughter.

'Of all things, and that's foremost on your mind? Charlie's been a good dog, but I've grown bored with him. I desire a new pet.'

While she'd been speaking I'd reached into the bag and taken out my gloves.

'I see,' I'd said as I slipped them on.

Enez seemed oblivious to my actions. She took a tube of skin cream, squeezed a dollop into the palm of her hand. After quickly rubbing them together she began to apply it to her neck and shoulders.

She paused and looked back at me. 'You shouldn't view our developing relationship as disagreeable, you'll find I'm capable of being a very generous mistress.'

Enez's face softened slightly. 'Let's look at the present situation realistically. Antoinette is going back to her parents within a few weeks. While I'm sure your time together has been delightful you both had to know it couldn't last forever. It's not like she can keep you hidden under her bed.' She'd almost succeeded in sounding sympathetic.

I'd bent my head down trying to appear submissive.

'I suppose you're right, but I'll need some time to adjust.'

'I understand, but you'll always have your memories. Now you and I are going to share some very interesting experiences.'

As Enez turned back around her elbow grazed a tube of lipstick, it fell off the dressing table and rolled under her feet. She muttered a curse as she pushed her chair back. She then bent forward as her hand blindly probed for the errant object.

I'd pulled the Walther from under my belt and quietly chambered a round. I then clicked off the safety, my arm was completely steady as I took aim.

When Enez finally located the lipstick I heard the sound of my voice.

'Enez, did you tell anyone I was coming over?'

She sat up

'No, why would …'

As the words were leaving her mouth I believe she'd already realized her grave error. But I wasn't about to allow that repugnant voice to utter another sound. I squeeze the trigger, my first shot pierced the right side of her back, thrusting her forward, the momentum was such that she went backward and along with the chair she landed on the floor. I stood up and looked down, Enez resembled a carelessly discarded marionette. I then noticed the red rose tattooed on the inner thigh of her left leg. I heard a noise, like a dog's chew toy and realized Enez was still breathing. I took a moment to look into her eyes before taking aim and firing a second bullet into her head. The mirror had finally shattered.

The stench of gunpowder caused my nose to twitch. I didn't linger over the corpse. I grabbed my bag and went into the bathroom across the hall. I placed the gun on the edge of the sink while I changed clothes; I kept my gloves on. After I placed everything including the gun into the bag I donned the baseball cap and slipped out of the bathroom.

Before I'd left I'd taken about 20 minutes to search Enez's belongings. I found her phone book along with a combination appointment book and ledger. I recognized some of the names in both but didn't find mine in either. Still, I knew they'd both have some value so I placed them in my bag. I also looked for a diary. Enez had seemed to be the type who would've kept one, but I found nothing.

Satisfied I'd left nothing incriminating I proceeded to make my exit. First I had to pass through the kitchen, down the steps onto a landing and out the back door into a small backyard.

None of Enez's neighbors were out and it seemed no one had been alerted by my gunfire. I calmly walked across the yard and hopped the chain link fence and into the alley. Still finding myself alone I turned left and proceeded down the alley until I reached a side street. After looking both ways and still seeing no one I started back toward the lot where I'd parked my car.

Five minutes later I was behind the wheel. Before returning home I made a single stop to a secluded canal where I deposited the disassembled Walther. The remainder of my drive I felt nothing but an overwhelming sense of tranquility. I'd slain the black widow, her quivering supplicants would have to find a new succubus to prostrate before.

Chapter Fifty One

When I returned home I felt light headed, yet I remained aware of the need for continued caution. Even though I hadn't come to the end of the road I still couldn't resist giving into my celebratory mood. I went into the kitchen and retrieved a bottle of champagne from the refrigerator. I heard the sound of the television coming from the next room. I took two glasses from the cupboard and carried them along with the bottle in the direction of the din.

Antoinette was sitting on the couch, her bare feet propped up on the coffee table. I didn't mind this act of indolence, powerless as I was at the sight of her sable skin and freshly lacquered toe nails. She was in the midst of watching Elizabeth Taylor and Montgomery Clift in black and white. It was an amazing coincidence and I couldn't help but grin. It was a film I was familiar with, I never could understand what Clift's character had seen in a simpering Shelly Winters.

I set the bottle and glasses down and Antoinette lept into my arms like I'd been a soldier returning from war, and hadn't I? She felt as light as a feather as I spun us around and we kissed. I sat myself down on the couch with her perched in my lap.

After we'd finished half the bottle Antoinette asked her one and only question.

'Where did it happen?'

'In her bedroom while she sat in front of her dressing table mirror.'

I looked into her eyes and realized she'd already known the answer.

But had I known what was on the horizon I would've treasured that night and the ones tha followed. Antoinette was about to be taken from me with a cruel abruptness.

Chapter Fifty Two

The following details I'd later learn in pieces. Enez's corpse was discovered five days after I'd killed her. I imagined she'd had a number of clients who'd been chagrined at being stood up, but not concerned enough to enquire as to her well-being.

The honor of discovery fell on, of all people, Christine. Apparently, the two had a lunch date, but when Enez failed to show and didn't return several phone calls Christine decided to investigate.

She gained entry through the back door, which I'd left unlocked. In an amusing twist Enez's air conditioner had stopped working, hastening her bodies putrification. Christine caught the stench, turned and ran back outside where, with the proper dramatic flourish, she fainted.

Hours later I received a distressful phone call from Christine, between spurts of hysteria she managed to convey being found and taken to the nearest hospital.

She'd already been questioned by police but hadn't yet been released. Charlie couldn't be located so she asked me to watch Antoinette and then informed me she'd already instructed her to go to my house.

After I set down the phone I turned to find Antoinette standing behind me.

'My aunt sent me over.'

'That was her on the phone.'

'I'm starving, may I have something to eat?'

I fixed her a turkey sandwich and heated a can of minestrone soup, she consumed the meal with the ferocity of a lumberjack.

An hour later Brenda Lee's voice filled the air as we laughed together on the floor, our bodies damp with sweat.

'I love you.'

She said it over and over, her resistance to the expression had vanished. It was after we'd tensed then relaxed for the final time that her tears had begun to flow. Heavy, vulnerable sobs that convulsed her body and shortened her breath. No matter how hard I implored her she still wouldn't reveal the source of her distress. But eventually she became quiet and rested her wet cheek against my chest. Moments later she fell into a deep sleep.

Her anguish had triggered a feeling of guilt in me. Antoinette Mouse, five foot, four inches and 15 years of age. How would our time together affect her in the future? Before I joined her in sleep I'd become convinced that between the two of us she would prevail.

Chapter Fifty Three

I awoke alone. Antoinette's scent clung to me and with it a feeling of melancholy. When I sat up I noticed the envelope propped on top of the stereo. I continued to stare at it for a long time before I finally rose to my feet and took it from its resting place. I sat down in the closest chair it was only after I could no longer forestall the inevitable that I finally summoned the courage to open it.

Inside was a single sheet of cream colored paper she'd folded in half. I held it with my fingertips as I read the lines of graceful script. It read:

My dearest Matthew,

I hope you will forgive me for my act of cowardice. I wanted to give you this news face to face, but couldn't. That is the reason I became so upset. As I write this you are sleeping only a few feet from me.

Last week Aunt Christine informed me that my parents had returned home early and had already sent my plane ticket. When you read this I will be among the clouds.

I should have told you, but I thought if I pushed it out of my mind it would somehow not make it so. I love you with my whole heart, before I left I gave you a final kiss, did you feel it?

Our only hope lies in the winter holidays, perhaps we can make some arrangements to be together. Maybe I can convince my parents to let me visit Aunt Christine. If not you could always ome to New York. These are the thoughts that will keep my days and nights bearable. Keep me close to your heart as I will be keeping you close to mine.

> I love you,
>
> Antoinette

Chapter Fifty Four

I wasn't accustomed to that kind of loss, delivered suddenly and penetrating. I'd allowed my friendships to wither and fall away. I'd already grown distant from my parents before their passing and my relationship with my sister had been tainted. I'd known, but always denied, that the day would come when Antoinette would have to return home, go back to school and the normal existence of a 15-year-old. But I'd fallen into the dual traps of sexual desire and emotional attachment.

In my blue fog I reread her letter several times and dwelled on her reference to the holidays. Was it a true ray of hope or her attempt to soften the blow? I pondered the few options left to us. Even if She could manage a return visit, how much time could we honestly expect to have? If I traveled to her it would take a great deal of subterfuge by both of us for even a brief meeting.

Still, after months of separation it would be worth any effort just to spend an hour with her. I told myself we'd find a way to be together again, even though at the time I had no way of contacting her. Antoinette had not included an address or phone number. Perhaps she'd worried that the information would've proven too tempting, and I had to admit that I might have done something foolish. Her father then would have been forced to do his daddy duty. I eventually put the letter down and went to fix myself a drink, it was the first of many. I sat outside on the patio and recalled that first afternoon when I laid eyes on my bronzed fawn.

Chapter Fifty Five

Enez's murder was, of course, investigated. I was never questioned, not even peripherally. I'd had a minor concern that someone may have witnessed our conversation at the LeLander, but no one came forward. It seemed its gloomy atmosphere had shielded me.

Charlie, however, wasn't spared from the machinations of the law. Upon hearing of Enez's demise his front dropped and out poured pronouncements of love for the witch. Upon witnessing this display Christine responded with typical feminine spite and made not so subtle implications to the police who took his despondence as a sign of a guilty conscience. They proceeded to put him through the ringer. All of this was related to me via a drunken phone call from none other than Christine herself.

Although Charlie's fingerprints were all over Enez's home the police failed to uncover further evidence and after the verification of his alibi he was released. Two weeks later Charlie disappeared. It was as if the earth had opened up and swallowed him.

Chapter Fifty Six

As September arrived I was still in possession of the items I'd taken from Enez's and I felt the time had come to get rid of them. I'd originally intended to mail them to Carpenter Gordon anonymously, but somehow it felt dishonest. Instead, I phoned him and arranged a meeting. I suggested Manner Park, it seemed appropriate. We'd agreed on a Monday afternoon when the park would be almost entirely empty.

I'd arrived 15 minutes early and found Carpenter sitting on a wooden bench waiting for me. He was dressed in a pale grey sweater, faded jeans and a pair of tan loafers. Yet, even in such casual attire he retained the air of quiet authority. He stood to greet me, we shook hands and then sat down.

I handed him the manila envelope that contained Enez's phonebook and ledger. I explained their significance but remained vague on how I'd come to obtain them. Carpenter briefly weighed the package in his hand before he set it down.

'You had us worried for a while, Matthew, we weren't sure you'd turn this over.

His statement hit me like a bucket of ice cold water, but Carpenter simply smiled at me.

'We'd been aware of Miss Sparrow for some time. She's not the first, it seems every few years some inquisitive whore attempts to sneak into our house. We'd been watching her for the past several weeks and were in the process of solving the problem. Imagine our surprise when we spotted you paying her a visit, on the night of her death no less. We really got curious when you exited through the rear dressed in a different set of clothes.

'I didn't see anyone.'

'Of course not.'

I looked down at my feet. 'I suppose I should've come to you first, but I felt I could deal with it myself. I wasn't even going to tell Anntoinnette, but she … '

'She already knew.'

I nodded. Carpenter put his hand on my shoulder. 'We didn't think you had it in you. Not that we thought you a coward, but your actions were unexpectedly bold.' He seemed almost proud of me.

'What happens now?' I'd asked, still unsure.

'To you, nothing. We have people in positions who will make sure the case of Miss Sparrow's death grows as cold as her corpse. We've already purged those who endangered us, but the material you've provided will be put to use, we can never be too careful. Does this put your mind at ease or do questions remain?'

I opened up like a dam and asked about the odd occurrences at Summer Isle, the wall and the figure I'd thought I'd seen. Could it have been Enez?'

'As to the wall, its origins and purpose are a mystery to all but our nymphs and those are secrets they don't share. Whatever this figure could have been, one thing is certain, it was not Miss Sparrow. She could have spent a millennia searching and she'd never been able to find Summer Isle. Neither had you without the aid of Antoinette.'

I didn't mention Eveswood, something told me Carpenter and the rest of the Bronze Peacock was unaware of its existence. When Carpenter said Antoinette's name I'd become overwhelmed with a fresh feeling of loss. He must have noticed my despondence.

'You miss her deeply.'

'Yes.'

'We sympathize, unfortunately it's all we have to offer and were afraid it won't be much help to you. You were allowed entry into another world, one you still may return to in time.

Carpenter picked up the envelope and rose to his feet.

"Take heart, Matthew, we have a feeling your separation from Antoinette is only temporary. It's a pity that the two of you will be unable to attend our winter solstice festivities. Perhaps next year.'

Carpenter smiled a final time and walked away. I remained sitting on that bench for some time and watched the path of the sun. I'd inventoried all my strange experiences of the past months. As I'd witnessed them I'd known they were mystical, but even that term seemed inadequate. Antoinette had touched my soul and had carried off a piece of it when she'd left. I sat on that bench and had never felt so alone.

Part Four
SEPTEMBER THROUGH JANUARY

Chapter Fifty Seven

The remainder of September was a mundane blur that'd flowed into October with little notice on my part. But in the early morning of October 30, Christine joined Enez in the hereafter. After her relationship with Charlie dissolved her alcoholism advanced and she'd added pills to the mix. I mostly witnessed her decline from afar.

What added a sense of the macabre was that Christine's death fell on what is known locally as 'Devil's Night' because of its notoriety as an arsonist's holiday. I'd later learn the cause of the fire was that after consuming a large quantity of alcohol and barbituates, Christine lit up a cigarette and then proceeded to pass out on her living room couch.

I was awoken along with most of my street, by the wailing of firetruck sirens. I became part of an audience who stood curbside in our pajamas and watched Christine's home as it was consumed in an inferno. Word of her immolation quickly spread amongst my neighbors.

I felt a pang of sadness for Christine. She hadn't deserved such a horrible fate. Without her act of hospitality, inviting her niece to spend the summer, I'd have never met Antoinette. For that fact alone she deserved to be mourned.

Chapter Fifty Eight

I'd accepted an offer from Passolini, in what turned out to be a feeble attempt to deal with my increasing despair. He was in the first week of shooting when I boarded a plane to his location in Prague. At the time I'd felt I needed to travel. My home had become a shrine to my misery. I missed Antoinette with an intensity that showed no signs of abating. I felt I needed something to keep me preoccupied.

I'd begun to regret my decision almost from the moment I stepped off the plane. The script I'd been asked to fix turned out to be the single worst thing Passolini would ever commit to film. The author was none other than Elton Highroad, he'd written it as a vanity project for his British girlfriend. She was an attractive woman, but hadn't possessed an ounce of acting skill. Volumes of time, money and takes were wasted under the weight of her insecurities and numerous times she'd stormed off set. The entire cast and crew grew to hate her. Passolini was powerless, he couldn't fire her. He was also trapped, he'd accepted a large advance and had already spent the lion's share.

The situation had already started deteriorating when I'd decided to stop coming to the set. Instead I began spending much of my time at a local tavern. The Enchanted Hunter was a stone's throw from the apartment I'd rented. I wrote pages that I knew Elton would reject. He hadn't hidden his contempt at my presence. I stopped writing and concentrated on drinking as much beer as possible. It wasn't long before I was on a first name basis with the owner. Passolini eventually discovered my hiding place, but by then he'd realized Elton had no intention of using my pages so he mostly left me alone.

One evening during dinner he broached the topic of Antoinette and with some reluctance I'd related the general details. Passolini then suggested a visit to one of the local brothels. It was a well-intentioned, but misguided piece of advice. But I held no resentment toward him, that'd been the only alms he'd had to offer.

When drinking I became maudlin, a sentimental pop song coming from an open window would send me into a daydream of revisited memories. They'd so take hold of my attention that more than once I wandered into traffic. It was only stupid, blind luck that prevented me from becoming a fatality. I finally decided to return to America, if I was going to be run over I wanted it to happen on my home soil.

Passolini practically begged me to stay, my company had been one of the few distractions from what had become a waking nightmare. I sympathized but knew I'd have to face Antoinette's absence. We either had a future together or were fated to be separated forever.

Chapter Fifty Nine

I'd just deboarded my plane and was walking towards the luggage carousel when I heard a voice call out.

'Matthew, hey Matthew!' It sounded with a desperate urgency.

I turned around to see Devon Shaun, a minor friend from college and one of the many I'd ignored over the summer. When he grabbed my hand he vigorously pumped it up and down as if he'd expected me to spout water, all the while sporting an overly broad grin.

I'd given him a brief once over. He was still the stout, short-haired man I'd remembered, while I no doubt resembled a rumpled, stubble-chinned mess.

'What've you been up to, still writing about rock bands?'

His voice seemed a few notches too loud, I attributed it as an after effect of the drinks I'd consumed during my flight.

He'd let go of my hand and launched into an account of finding himself, 'In your neck of the woods and had decided to stop by.'

The statement annoyed me. With the exception of Antoinette I'd always disliked unannounced visitations. Devon continued, he'd believed me to be home because he'd heard music coming from inside.

'I rang the bell and knocked on the door, but no one answered.'

I imagined Antoinette, lying on her stomach, her legs moving up and down in time with the music and blissfully ignoring Devon's unwanted intrusion.

He invited me to join him for a drink, but I begged off. We concluded our meeting with mutual promises to stay in touch. I, of course, had no intention of doing so. There seemed to be no end to my lies and misdeeds.

Chapter Sixty

I'd just returned from a trip to the post office where I'd claimed three week's worth of unopened mail. I deposited the bundle onto the kitchen table and my attention was immediately caught by a pale blue envelope. I knew instantly it was from Antoinette. My hand trembled as I picked it up. There was a post office box listed as the return address. I took a butter knife from a drawer and carefully sliced open the envelope. Inside was a single sheet of matching stationery.

My dearest Matthew,

A thousand apologies for not writing to you sooner. I wanted to make sure I had a safe place to receive your responses, otherwise you'd have gotten a hundred letters by now.

It was terrible what happened to Aunt Christine. Despite some of the things I'd said she'd always treated me with kindness and I will truly miss her. My parents had her remains sent here. I visited her grave site the other day and said goodbye.

But I miss you all the more. At night I lie in my bed letting my hands wander and imagining they're yours. But it doesn't always work and I dissolve into tears. My pillow has absorbed so much of my sadness.

I'm able to find some distraction at school, but even there my attention is distracted to memories of our time together. My friends have remarked about my moodiness, but how can I explain what I'm feeling? I know they'd never understand.

I've included a picture with the letter, I hope you like it. It occurred to me the other day that I don't have a single one of you, how can this be? I hope you will send me one, you needn't worry, I've a very good hiding place. Write me back soon and let me know if you miss me even a little bit.

I love you,

Antoinette

I walked into the next room and sat down. I gazed at the photograph she'd enclosed. Annntoinette was seated on a stone bench in front of a wrought iron fence, she was dressed in her school uniform. She wore a green cardigan over a white blouse, a tie knotted at her buttoned collar. Her legs were pressed together under her tartan skirt and tilted slightly to the left. On her feet she wore white ankle socks and black slippers with a single strap. Although her tan had faded her skin still radiated health and vibrance. But even though she was wearing a smile I could see the sadness in her eyes.

I imagined what it would be like to be her classmate. To watch as she walked down the hall, books pressed against her chest. To sit beside her in class, her pink legs crossing and uncrossing, me trying to guess the color of her underwear. How I'd take her to some secluded spot where I could press my lips against hers whil I probed under her skirt until her breathing became pensive.

Once I'd managed to collect myself I set about crafting a response. I reassured her that I loved her as ardently as ever and that I missed her desperately. I concluded with a promise that I'd find some way for us to be together again and fulfilled her request for a photograph.

While driving to a mailbox I'd absent-mindedly turned on the radio. 'Ruby Tuesday' came over the air and I felt myself overcome with emotion. I was forced to pull the car over into an empty lot until the storm passed.

Chapter Sixty One

Antoinette and I continued to correspond. With each letter we grew increasingly passionate and desparate.

I'd begun using my collection of photos during self-gratification, but they ultimately proved to be an inadequate substitute for the flesh and blood Antoinette, so I ceased the practice.

Chapter Sixty Two

In the first days of December I received a letter from Antoinette. Between her amorous pronouncements and the more mundane information was a pair of lines I found troubling.

'I've noticed a well-dressed, middle-aged man hanging around my school, always directly across the street. For some reason he seems familiar, like someone we may have met over the summer.'

There'd been only one occasion where Antoinette and I would've had an opportunity to meet anyone, the Bronze Peacock's coronation ball. Since our last conversation I'd decided to distance myself from Carpenter and the organization.

I had several reasons for doing this. The most obvious being that since Antoinette had returned home I'd no longer had a reason to retain contact. I'd come to the conclusion that the group was much larger and far-reaching than I'd originally thought. I'd also come to believe that Charlie's disappearance was linked to them, that they'd drawn the logical conclusion that Enez had possibly shared her knowledge of the group with him. That would've made Charlie, in Carpenter's words, a loose end. I had no tangible proof to support my conclusions, just my gut feelings, which seemed like enough.

I'd also begun to take the time to thoroughly recount my summer with Antoinette and the series of extraordinary events that ran the course of those months. Her ability to move silently, her pronounced intuition, my dreams, the black out at the coronation, Summer Isle, Eveswood, and finally, her ritual on the eve of my killing Enez.

Antoinette had called her a witch, I'd seen evidence of her being one while I'd been in her home. Enez had poisoned Antoinette, but why? Had she recognized something in her she'd wanted to possess, and had Carpenter as well?

I'd taken to studying the stories of the nureids, or nymphs and was confronted by a simple truth. My Antoinette was indeed the myth made flesh, and she'd been completely aware of this.

Nymphs were generally regarded as divine beings who animated nature. Enez wanted to take Antoinette's power and so did the Bronze Peacock, to what end I could only guess.

Carpenter knew I'd killed Enez. Was the fact that he'd had this leverage against me the reason I was still breathing?

Chapter Sixty Three

I'd begun to remain, for the most part, indoors. The shades drawn shut, the phone disconnected. I'd wander about my home, at times I thought I saw Antoinette out of the coner of my eye, but there would be no one when I turned to address her image. There were also many nights when I'd be awaken and swore I could feel her lying beside me. But when I reached over I felt only cold emptiness.

As Christmas neared I revived a custom from my childhood. I'd drive around my neighborhood and look at the various displays of holiday lights. I still remembered how my father would gather the entire family into our car and we'd set out on a nocturnal tour. The combination of colored lights, plastic Santas and nativity scenes had cast a magical glow on the world. Alison and I held hands as we stared out the car window at a landscape that seemed other worldly.

That solitary activity was only a sliver of warmth in what had become a barren existence. As the date of Antoinette's birth approached I imagined her dress in her winter coat, a scarf around her neck, her cheeks rosey from the cold. I'd stay out for about an hour before returning to my own home, which stood dark and without decoration.

Chapter Sixty Four

On December 21, I received a phone call from Carpenter Gordon. He asked id I'd be willing to meet him at a local bar that was located only five blocks from my home.

'How does six o'clock sound?' he asked.

I agreed. Coincidentally, I'd been planning an outing of some sort. I'd begun to realize that my self-imposed isolation wasn't healthy. Perhaps the holiday season had been having an effect.

I'd left the house at 5:30, because the weather was agreeable I'd decided to walk. Outside was cold, but not unpleasantly so. The air was clear and still. The ground was covered with a thin layer of snow, it reminded me of powdered sugar.

As I walked off the remaining minutes of sun light it occurred to me that I'd heard something in Carpenter's voice that hadn't been present in our previous conversations. It'd been as if his usual ease and confidence had been tapped down. I'd actually known very little about the man. What did he do for a living, did he have a wife and children? Was it possible he had no family and was simply suffering the holiday blues. Perhaps I'd been the first one called who'd picked up the phone.

When I'd reached the intersection of White Tower and Harrison I was greeted by the familiar sight of the Buffalo Nickel saloon. It was a neighborhood staple, first opened when I was a small child and still run by the original owners. The last time I'd patronized the place had been shortly before I'd left on my first trip overseas.

I noticed it still lacked the usual signage, but maintained the same mural painted on the side of the building. I felt a certain reassurance in the never-changing landmark. After I'd looked both ways and saw no traffic I then jogged across the street.

I entered and was immediately struck by the simultaneous rush of warmth and intermingling conversations. The interior was small, a bar that ran the length of the right side with four booths on the left. There was barely enough room for the pool table and juke box. The atmosphere was decidedly cozy, no doubt the reason for its continued popularity.

I'd spotted Carpenter instantly, he was sitting at the far end of the bar and nursing a whiskey. Even from across the room I could read the faint apprehension on his face.

Bing Crosby had already begun crooning 'White Christmas' as I made my way toward him. When we shook hands I noticed his palm was damp.

'So glad you could make it. Having a nice holiday I hope,' he said smiling, even that had dimmed.

'As much as I'm able.' I motioned to the bartender. I ordered a pint of stout then removed my coat and draped it over the back of my stool. Carpenter never took his eyes off me and he silently paid for my drink.

I'd just settled into my seat when he asked, 'Have you heard from Antoinette lately?'

It was not a question I'd expected and it didn't explain his current behavior. I'd let it hang in the air as I took my first sip of beer. I took a moment to enjoy the flavor before I finally responded.

'As a matter of fact, we've been corresponding regularly. Of course, it doesn't compare with having her physically present.'

'Yes, I imagine you miss each other terribly.'

'You've no idea, or perhaps you do.'

Carpenter swirled his drink as he grew more forlorn.' I haven't been able to spend much time with Valerie as of late, it's the same every fall and winter. But that's not why I asked to see you.'

I didn't fail to notice Carpenter had been referring to himself in the singular. That had been a first.

'There hasn't been an unseen complication concerning a certain Miss Sparrow?'

'Oh no, as far as we're concerned that situation has been resolved.'

Carpenter's eyes began to scan the room and he seemed reluctant to bring the reason behind his invitation. I'd found myself becoming annoyed. I'd arrived in high spirits and he was dampening them with each passing moment.

'So, what is on your mind?' I'd said, not completely hiding my irritation.

'We want to apologize.'

'I don't understand.'

Carpenter downed the remainder of his glass then signaled for another round for both of us, even though my own drink was only half finished. I saw this as stalling. After the drinks arrived he continued.

'Last time we spoke we made mention of our winter solstice celebration.'

'I remember.'

'Matthew, are you at all aware of what Antoinette represents?'

'Yes, I've had a great deal of time to think about it. Have you ever heard of a place called 'Eveswood?''

'No.' I could tell by his tone and the expression on his face that he hadn't. But before he could ask me to elaborate I interjected.

'You were saying.'

'Well, it would've been a unique opportunity to have the both of you attend, as we've never had anyone as exceptional as Antoinette. It would've made things more than simply symbolic. Of course this only could have been arranged after discussing it with the both of you. We're afraid one of our members attempted to take things into his own hands.'

I instantly recalled Antoinette's letter, which mentioned the strange man loitering outside of her school. I grabbed Carpenter by the arm, hard enough that he winced.

'What have you done?' I said through clinched teeth.

Carpenter shrank back like a frightened child. 'Nothing, nothing at all. She hasn't been harmed in any way, we want to assure you of that. As we said this man acted independently and without authorization.'

I released him and he downed his second drink in one swallow.

'The situation resolve itself, but we're worried we may have angered Antoinette. We were hoping you could explain, let her know we meant no offense. We've always prided ourselves on scrupulously taking precautions against causing any malice towards the nereids.'

With some effort I managed a smile. 'She hasn't mentioned any offending incidences. Perhaps your worries are unfounded.'

'We certainly hope so. Still, would you pass along our sincerest apologies?'

'Of course.'

Carpenter finally seemed to relax and with a little prompting from me we moved on to other topics. We both stayed another two hours and got along like old friends. But I'd made a mental note to get Antoinette's side of the story ad to further distance myself from Carpenter and the organization. What could have possibly happened to throw such fear into a group of grown men?

Chapter Sixty Five

It was on the 23rd that I received a Christmas card from Antoinette. I didn't open it immediately, instead I waited until after sunset. First, I built a fire, poured myself a whiskey and settled into the leather chair that had been my father's favorite. The front of the card was illustrated with the image of a decorated spruce with toys gathered around its base. Above the tree were the words 'Merry Christmas' written in elaborate calligraphy. Antoinette's longhand covered every inch of the card's interior.

My dearest Matthew,

For many this is one of the happiest times of the year, and to the outside world, all with me is well. But there's only one thing that could raise my spirits. My thoughts keep returning to Summer Isle, how it felt like we were the only two people on earth, happy and needing no one but each other.

Why are we continuing to deny ourselves, surely there's someplace in this world where we can be together. Will you come for me? I would follow you anywhere. You needn't send me your answer. Instead, I'll wait. On the morning of January third you'll find me outside, packed and ready to go wherever you wish.

I love you,

Antoinette

P.S. I'm adopted. I don't know why I didn't tell you earlier. My mother died giving birth to me and I've never met my biological father.

The final line was her home address.

There it was, clear as crystal. I'd always known there'd be a share of risk, but what choice did I really have? My life had grown unbearable without her.

The next day, Christmas Eve, I awoke early. There was much to do and very little time. The first thing I needed to do was to buy a map of New York State.

Chapter Sixty Six

It was the early morning hours of January 4. I laid in my bed naked and staring at the ceiling. Antoinette and I had just concluded a very rigorous physical reunion. I listened to the sound of running water coming from the bathroom where Antoinette was rinsing the excess dye from her hair.

On the morning of January 3, I'd left my motel room before sunrise and driven to the address Antoinette had provided. I pulled up to a two-story brick colonial and found her waiting for me. A single suitcase was all she had with her.

I'd exited the car, as I walked to her all I could hear was the sound of snow crunching under my feet. Antoinette dropped her suitcase and ran into my arms. There was only time for a single kiss, her lips were dry, but warm.

We drove without stopping, Antoinette pressed close to me. We spoke little, when I'd asked her about the man outside her school Antoinette simply told me he'd been hit by a car. I didn't pursue the matter any further.

I'd accomplished much in the days that'd proceeded. I'd been able to secure new identification for the both of us, selected a destination and had made our travel arrangements. Antoinette liked my choice of Rio de Janero, I made sure to pick someplace warm.

Of course it's helped that I'd had more than a few people to aid and abet me. Passolini, of course, and Carpenter was more than willing to bend over backwards, he didn't want to risk Antoinette's ire.

She walked out of the bathroom, naked and toweling of her hair that she'd colored a chocolate brown. She paused in front of the mirror to evaluate her new look.

'Not bad, but I'm going back to blonde as soon as possible.'

She tossed the towel aside and climbed into bed, planting a kiss on my lips before resting her head on my chest.

Yes, I thought, very soon my Antoinette, freshly sweet sixteen will once again be restored to her blonde and bronzed majesty. We'll be far from America and beginning anew. Nothing would separate us ever again.

The End

Made in the USA
Charleston, SC
12 June 2014